Emily Windsnap

AND THE FALLS OF
FORGOTTEN ISLAND

Liz Kessler

Orion

First published in Great Britain in 2018 by
Hodder and Stoughton

1 3 5 7 9 10 8 6 4 2

Text © Liz Kessler, 2018
Illustrations © Lisa Horton, 2018

The moral rights of the author have been asserted.

A CIP catalogue record for this book
is available from the British Library.

ISBN 978 1 5101 0232 3

Printed and bound in Great Britain by Clays Ltd, St Ives plc

The paper and board used in this book are from
well-managed forests and other responsible sources.

MIX
Paper from
responsible sources
FSC® C104740

Orion Children's Books
An imprint of
Hachette Children's Group
Part of Hodder and Stoughton
Carmelite House
50 Victoria Embankment
London EC4Y 0DZ

An Hachette UK Company

www.hachette.co.uk
www.hachettechildrens.co.uk
www.lizkessler.co.uk

Dedication

I'm writing this in the aftermath of a bombing in Manchester, UK, a city where I lived for twenty years. The youngest fatality was eight years old, and as I write this, many other children are still in hospital.

Like all the books in the Emily Windsnap series, this book is about different communities who think they have nothing in common finding ways to overcome their differences and learning to live together, work together and create harmony.

In this context, and with a firm belief that the next generation has the power to do good things with this beautiful world of ours, I am dedicating this book to all those who work in their communities to help others, and to those who believe that spreading love, kindness and empathy will eventually win the day.

And I'm taking this opportunity to share a phrase I've loved for nearly thirty years.

"Practise random kindness and senseless acts of beauty."

Liz Kessler, 5th June, 2017

PROLOGUE

*T*he first sign of trouble was the rain.

Rain that fell like a river. Like a torrent. Like an avalanche crashing down with such ferocity some thought it would split the earth in two. Others argued the earth could not break, but that it might perhaps be drowned.

Most didn't argue at all. They ran. They hid. They protected themselves and their families as well as they could, waiting out a storm the likes of which no one had ever seen before.

The likes of which no one would have thought possible.

The likes of which, surely, could only have been created by magic. Nothing of this earth could produce such ferocity.

The rain continued on and on, as hours spilled into days. It fell into the ocean with such relentless force that the sea levels rose. It swirled across swells, rising into mountainous peaks; drilled down into whirlpools; darkened the sky so that it seemed the rain had even drowned the sun.

And then, like a hungry shark closing in on its prey, like a wizard finding the perfect ingredient for his spell, the rain zoned in on what it was looking for: the island in the centre of the ocean. The island with no more than a hundred inhabitants.

The rain wanted only *one* of them.

Elsewhere, the sky lightened. But not above this island. Above the island, it seemed all the darkness of the world, the darkness of a thousand nights, the darkness of the most tortured soul, was gathered together into one cloud.

The cloud was now so large, it was as if the very fabric of space had opened up to swallow the island whole.

For a moment, the world held its breath.

And then the cloud erupted. Like a giant dragon breathing fire, the darkness unleashed its demons upon the island. Down they rained, sparks flying across the sky like fireworks as the spell was cast.

The rain poured so hard into the centre of the

island, it drilled a hole all the way through it.

Enormous arrows of rain continued to pour down all around, so hard that the island's edges were beaten and hewn into rough, ragged cliffs. Gigantic jagged teeth that refused to let anyone in or out of the land beyond them.

Tides rose: huge, angry swells that it seemed would never again become calm.

Eventually, the cloud reached the final side of the island. The longest, straightest edge.

The first cannonball of rain crashed against the foot of the cliffs so hard it dented the cliff itself.

The second punched a hole above the first. Three more times the cloud fired explosions of water at the cliff, higher and higher, as if it were chasing its prey to the top.

Who was the prey, though?

The people retreated as the balls of water crashed into their land. Each explosion sent them deeper and deeper into the island's hidden forest, forced them into shelters, contained them in clearings and caves.

There were those who saw a large figure rising out of the water – a figure of giant, contorted proportions.

There were those who heard words streaking through the air.

'. . . Betrayed me . . .'

'. . . We had a deal . . .'

'. . . Never forgive . . .'

The words grew softer as the rain climbed higher and higher up the mountain beyond the cliffs.

As the rain slowed, the cloud took moisture from the fierce swells, growing and growing so that soon, the entire island was hidden inside the cloud.

Eventually, the sky beyond the island cleared. It was over.

All that was left was a fierce swell, an island cut to shreds and a thick blanket of fog surrounding it. An angry, raging waterfall screamed down the cliff side, forming a deadly barrier to the bay behind it.

Those who had survived crept out of their hiding places to find they were now trapped on the island by the cliffs and the falls. Closed off from the world. Forgotten. Abandoned.

And for more than five hundred years, that was how it stayed.

CHAPTER 1

'*E*mily, are you listening to me?'
My best friend's voice jolted me so hard I jumped and splashed myself in the face. 'What? What?' I spluttered. 'Sorry, I must have dozed off.'

'Ha!' Shona said with a laugh. 'I'm clearly not very interesting!'

'No!' I protested. 'You are! Of course you are. I'm just . . .'

'You're exhausted.' Shona finished my sentence for me.

'I am a bit,' I admitted. 'Sorry.'

5

'Don't be,' Shona said. 'Your life has been manic lately. I'm surprised you're still in one piece.'

Shona was right. We'd recently come home from a geography field trip that had been the latest in a long line of adventures.

'I barely am,' I said. 'I mean, can you actually think of more than a week at a time when I wasn't being almost squeezed to death by a sea monster or getting trapped with sirens in a forgotten underwater cave, or dodging hammerhead sharks to get my dad out of Neptune's underwater prison?'

Shona flicked her tail as she swam up to the water's edge. Shona's a mermaid. Kind of like I am, except she's a full-time one. I'm only a mermaid when I go in water. I'm an ordinary girl the rest of the time.

We were hanging out at Rainbow Rocks, our special place.

'Well, yes,' Shona replied. 'There was the time when you escaped from Neptune's evil brother in the frozen Arctic. You weren't doing any of those things then.'

I laughed. 'Exactly. And to top it off, we go on a school trip where the most exciting activity is *meant* to be studying local rock formations, and what happens? I discover a spooky underwater ship and have to rescue a boat full of people who are trapped in the mysterious land of Atlantis!'

Shona smiled as she swished her tail, spreading

droplets of water in a sparkly arc above the sea. 'Craziness!' she said. 'You need a break.'

'I probably do,' I admitted. 'Just a little one. What are the chances that will happen?'

Shona frowned. 'Hmm. Slim. It is *you* we're talking about, here.'

I splashed water at her and she laughed and ducked under the surface.

'It's true though,' Shona went on. 'You're addicted to adventures – you just can't resist them.'

'I don't do it on purpose,' I protested. '*They* come to *me!*'

'Yeah,' Shona agreed. 'You're like an adventure magnet.' She swam around me towards a large, smooth rock and pulled herself on to it. Her tail flicking in the water, she perched on the edge of the rock and ran a hand through her hair, squeezing sea water out of it and patting it down into neat strands.

Shona's one of those mermaids who cares about things like her hair. Before she met me, she wanted to be a siren – you know, the whole sitting on a rock, singing beautiful songs and luring fishermen to watery graves thing. She feels differently now that humans and merfolk are a bit more aware of each other, but she still likes to look good. Me, I don't care so much. I just like to have fun. Trouble is, my fun usually ends up as . . . well, trouble.

'Now I think about it,' Shona went on, 'what do

all these adventures have in common? Or, should I say, *who* do they have in common? Other than you.'

I thought for a moment. 'I guess *you've* been by my side in most of them.'

'Exactly.' Shona smoothed her hair and slid back into the sea. 'And so I think I am qualified to tell you that I am officially declaring both of us in need of some downtime, before we collapse in a heap of jellyfish goo. I am completely adventured-out and so are you. Let's swill out for a while.'

'Swill out?'

Shona shrugged. 'Like chill out. But in water. Come on, let's make a deal. Let's try to be boring for a while. Time out. No more adventures.'

I thought for a moment. 'OK. Let's do it. No more adventures.'

Shona flicked her tail to push herself upright in the water and indicated for me to face her and do the same. She held a hand up. 'You too,' she said.

I swished my tail and held my right hand up, palm facing hers.

'OK, repeat after me,' she said. 'I, Emily Windsnap.'

I cleared my throat. 'I, Emily Windsnap,' I repeated, trying not to laugh.

'Do solemnly declare.'

'Do solemnly declare.'

'That I shall not be tempted by adventures, risks or mysteries for at least one month.'

'That I shall not be tempted by adventures, risks or mysteries for at least one month.'

Shona raised an eyebrow. 'Think you can do it?'

'I am *desperate* to do it,' I replied.

'Swishy!' she replied. 'Bring on the boring.'

I grinned as we slapped hands in a watery high five. 'Bring on the boring!'

Shona had gone back to her family in Shiprock. That's the merfolk town under the sea near us. I was swimming home for dinner.

I live on a boat in Brightport with my mum and dad. Mum lives on the upper deck of the boat, as she's a human. I do too, when I'm being a human and spending time with Mum. I also like to hang out in the lower deck with Dad. That part is under the water because Dad's a merman, so it's how we manage to all live together.

I pulled myself out of the sea and perched on the edge of the boat. As I sat there, I watched my tail flicker and shimmer. Droplets of water sprinkled off the end of it, glinting in the late afternoon sun. Then, gradually, my tail stiffened up, straightened out and began to tingle. Finally, it disappeared altogether as my legs came back.

You'd think I'd be used to it by now. I first discovered that I become a mermaid when I go in water just over a year ago, when I was twelve. It still amazes me every time it happens.

I leaned over the side of the boat to squeeze the water out of my hair. Then I went inside.

Mum and her best friend Millie were huddled together on the sofa, flicking through magazines.

'Hi, sweet pea,' Mum said as I came in. 'Nice time?'

'Yep. Swishy,' I said. *Swishy* is Shona's favourite word – but I like using it too. It makes me feel like a real mermaid.

'That's nice, darling,' Mum replied.

'What're you doing?' I called over my shoulder to them as I went into the galley and poured myself a drink of orange squash.

'Looking through holiday brochures,' Millie replied airily.

'Really?' I took my drink and went to join them in the saloon. 'I didn't know we were going on holiday.'

'We're not,' Mum said.

'Yes, you are,' Millie countered.

I stared at Millie. She glanced up and stared back. 'Your mum's got SAD,' she said with a meaningful look in her eyes. Millie does most things with a meaningful look of some sort. You learn to ignore it after a while.

'What are you sad about, Mum?' I asked. 'Has something happened to Dad? Are you OK?'

Mum waved an arm at me. 'I'm fine!' she said. 'I'm not sad at all.'

'But Millie said—'

'I said she's *got* SAD, not she *is* sad,' Millie interrupted.

'Oh,' I said. 'I see.' I didn't actually see at all. I squeezed on to the sofa next to Mum. 'Actually, what exactly is the difference?'

Millie sighed. 'S–A–D,' she spelled out. 'Seasonal Affective Disorder. I've been reading about it. Your mum is exhausted and drained.'

'Is she?' I asked. 'Are you, Mum?'

Mum shrugged. 'I suppose I am a bit,' she conceded.

They sounded like me and Shona. Hadn't we just been saying pretty much the same thing? Maybe I had this SAD thing too.

'Can it be treated?' I asked. 'What can we do about it?'

Millie held up one of the holiday brochures they were looking at. 'WINTER SUN' it said in big letters on the front page.

'Sunshine,' she said. 'That's what your mum needs.' Then she squinted and pushed her reading glasses up her nose. 'In fact, you're looking a bit on the pasty side too, Emily. A bit of winter sun wouldn't do you any harm either.'

Just then, I heard a swooshing noise underneath us. 'Dad!' I yelled. Dad had been working on building new caves with some of the merfolk in Shiprock. The swooshing meant he was home from work.

A moment later, he popped his head through the trapdoor that links the boat's two floors.

Mum got up and went over to him. 'Hi, darling,' she said, bending down to kiss him. 'How was your day?'

'It was swishy!' Dad said, glancing across to wink at me. 'And you know the best news of all?'

'What's that?' Mum asked.

'They're giving us all the week after next off.'

'Oh, that's wonderful,' Mum said. 'You can spend the week at home with us.' She moved to stand up again and snagged her trousers on a broken floorboard. Then she glanced around the boat and nodded her head towards the table in the middle of the saloon, propped up by a pile of books in place of its missing leg. 'Maybe we can use the time to get a few jobs done around the place.'

'Sounds like a barrel-load of fun,' Dad said with a grimace.

'Wait. The week after next? That's my half term, isn't it?' I asked.

'Sure is, little 'un,' Dad replied.

Millie slammed her brochure shut and pursed her lips. 'Well, that settles it,' she said firmly.

'Forget your little jobs around the place. I'll move in and get to work on them for you while you go and enjoy yourselves.'

Mum's face fell. Millie might be her best friend, but she's not exactly the most practical person in the world. If you left your to-do list in her hands, there'd be a fairly strong chance that she'd turn the list into a floaty scarf and try to hypnotise the jobs into doing themselves. 'Honestly, Millie,' Mum said carefully, 'you really don't have to do—'

Millie held up a hand to stop her. 'I'm insisting on it. And it's not just me insisting.'

I looked around. 'Um. There's no one else saying anything,' I pointed out.

Millie gave me one of those knowing looks and, lowering her voice, she said, 'Serendipity herself has intervened.'

'Seren — what?' I asked.

Millie impatiently shook her head. 'Serendipity. Synchronicity. Coincidence. Call it what you will. It's all coming together. Your half term, your mother's needs and your father's time off.' She held up her brochure and waved it in the air. 'You're going on holiday, the lot of you. Fate has decreed it.'

Dad looked at Mum. 'Millie's right,' he said. 'We could *all* do with some time off.' With a wink, he added, 'And if fate has decreed it, who are we to argue?' He held a hand out to Millie. 'Come on, then,' he said. 'Pass me one of those. Let's book ourselves a holiday!'

It was later that day, and Mum, Dad, Millie, Aaron and I were flicking through brochures.

Aaron's my boyfriend. He's a semi-mer like me – the only one I know, of my age anyway.

Mum and Millie were on the sofa, pointing at pictures and mumbling, 'Oooh, look at that,' and 'What about this one?' and 'Oh, my!' every other minute.

Dad was leafing through his with increasing impatience.

Aaron and I were sitting on a beanbag looking at one together, but mostly using it as an excuse to huddle up close. I leaned into him as I turned the pages.

'Look at the colour of the water!' Aaron exclaimed as I turned a page.

'Check out the size of the pool,' I added, pointing at the hotel as Aaron pulled me closer to look at the picture.

A couple of minutes later, Dad closed the last of his brochures and sighed loudly. 'This is stupid,' he said. We'd been looking through the brochures for the last hour. 'There's *nothing* in here that we can do together.'

Dad was right. We couldn't exactly go to some high-rise hotel for a holiday together. Dad would have to spend the whole week in the swimming pool. It would be like us going on holiday and him being kept in an aquarium!

'Wait!' Millie suddenly rose from the sofa.

Dad stopped still. I put my brochure down, Aaron froze, and Mum looked up. We all stared at Millie as she waved her brochure in the air.

'I've got it!' she announced. 'I've found the perfect place for your holiday.' Millie held the brochure out to me. 'Show your dad, go on.'

I dragged myself out of the beanbag and got up to take the brochure from Millie. Studying the pictures, I made my way across the boat.

'The Tiptoe Hotel at Majesty Island', the page read.

I didn't read any more of the words. I was too busy looking at the pictures. The bluest, clearest water I'd ever seen, the most golden sand you could imagine, and a line of little huts stretching out from the beach into the bay.

I passed the brochure to Dad. Mum got up from the sofa and came to join us.

'Majesty Island,' Dad murmured. 'Sounds grand.'

'Listen to this,' Mum said, reading aloud over Dad's shoulder. '"Majesty Island is a small island oozing with natural riches and wonders. With the softest golden sand, and the bluest, clearest sea, it is a jewel in the middle of the ocean. A place where you will definitely feel like royalty."'

Aaron joined us and read aloud from further down the page: "'Wake up to the sound of the sea, and within seconds, you can slip into the sparkling waters of Bluefin Bay."'

'It sounds incredible,' I said.

'It does. You have to go!' Aaron said. Then he grabbed my hand and whispered, 'Even though I'll miss you like crazy.'

'Me too,' I whispered back.

Dad looked at Mum. 'It does sound romantic,' he said.

Mum did that gooey smile back at Dad that she does sometimes. 'It really does.'

Which, yeah, might be nice for them. But if this was going to be some kind of second honeymoon, I didn't really want to play gooseberry.

But maybe I didn't have to. And perhaps I didn't have to miss Aaron.

'Mum, Dad, can Aaron and Shona come too?' I asked. The thought of spending a week with my two favourite people was probably the most perfect thing I could imagine.

'*Two* friends? I don't know,' Mum said. 'No offence, Aaron, but I thought the whole idea was that it would be a relaxing holiday for me. Looking after three children doesn't sound like much of a break.'

Aaron waved his hands in front of him. 'It's fine, honestly, don't worry about it,' he said.

Millie loudly cleared her throat. 'Sorry, don't mind me,' she said, thumping her chest.

'You wouldn't have to look after us,' I said to Mum. 'We'd hang out together all the time! And we'd leave you guys to be all soppy and romantic.'

Dad laughed as he stole a quick kiss on Mum's cheek. 'Sounds good to me,' he said.

Mum sighed. 'Oh, I don't know,' she said.

Millie coughed again, even more loudly this time. Mum turned to look at her. 'You OK, Millie?'

'What, me? Oh, yes, I'm fine,' Millie replied airily. 'Just a tickle.' She picked up another magazine and, as she nonchalantly flicked through it, she added, 'I always get a bit of a virus this time of year. It's just the weather. I'll be fine, though. Don't worry about me. You carry on with your plans.'

Mum laughed. 'Millie! I thought you wanted to stay and look after the boat?'

'What? Oh, yes. That's right. Go on, you get on with your planning. Ignore me.' She coughed once more and pulled her scarf up to cover her throat.

'I suppose . . .' Dad said. 'If we had a third adult

there, it would be someone else to watch the kids.'

'Dad's right,' I said to Mum. If Millie joining us meant more chance of my friends coming too, then I was all for it. 'Plus you'd have someone to keep you company if Dad wanted to take us on any underwater trips.' I turned to Aaron. 'You'd like to go out exploring beautiful, jewel-like waters with Dad, wouldn't you?'

Aaron's eyes were wide. 'Errr, yes!'

'That is a good point,' Mum agreed. She turned to Millie. 'OK, Millie, do you want to come?'

Millie slammed down her brochure and pulled her scarf off her neck. 'Count me in,' she beamed. 'Wouldn't miss it for the world.'

Dad laughed. 'Right,' he said. 'I'll talk to Shona's parents. Aaron, ask your mum. If everyone agrees to it, then yes, all right, we'll book it.'

I squeezed Aaron's hand as he got up to leave. 'Hope she says yes,' I said.

'She will,' Aaron replied. 'I'll make sure of it.'

I looked at the pictures again as Dad and Aaron left. It looked so beautiful. The perfect place to do what Shona had said and 'swill out'. A week of doing nothing. No adventures, no mysteries, no anything. Just lying around in the sunshine, swimming whenever we felt like it and not having a care in the world.

It was going to be the most perfect week of my life.

CHAPTER 2

'Wow – look at it!' Shona said. All around us was nothing but twinkling turquoise water, stretching out as far as the eye could see.

I could hardly believe it had all happened so quickly. The hotel had some cheap deals as it was a last-minute booking. Shona and Aaron's parents had agreed, and now we were really here. Majesty Island.

Mum had spoken to the hotel manager. He had never met a mermaid or merman in real life, but he'd read about sightings of merpeople and was totally open to us coming. He even put us in a couple of the rooms that had underwater caves directly below them.

And here we were. In paradise.

Our rooms were little chalets on stilts in the water. Each one had its own balcony, and below the decking of our balconies were the underwater caves the hotel had told us about. We could dive off and swim straight down into the caves.

Aaron had one room, with Dad staying in the cave below it. I had another, with Shona in the cave below mine, and Mum and Millie were sharing a third one next to mine, with an adjoining door in between.

I was sitting on my balcony now, legs dangling over the edge as Shona swam below me. Little steps led straight into the water, which was so clear I could see the rocky formation of Shona's cave underneath.

'Want to explore?' Shona asked with a smile.

I laughed. 'Do you?'

She pulled a face at me. 'Look at it. Of course I do!'

'OK, let's do it,' I said, stepping back into my room. I threw my case on the bed and opened it. 'I'll get my swimming stuff!'

Just then, there was a knock at my door.

'It's open!' I called.

A second later, the door opened and Aaron came

in. He took my hand and pulled me back out on to the balcony. 'Look at this place!' he exclaimed.

'I know. Beautiful isn't it?'

'Like you,' Aaron said and squeezed my hand.

I laughed. Mainly to hide my embarrassment. I mean, I liked him saying things like that, but I didn't want Shona to feel left out by it. She had a boyfriend too, but he worked for Neptune and she hardly ever got to see him.

'Do you two just want to be together?' Shona asked.

I pulled my hand away from Aaron's. 'No! Course not.' I turned to Aaron. 'We were just about to go out swimming,' I said. 'You coming?'

'Yeah!' Aaron looked between me and Shona. 'I mean, as long as you don't mind?'

'Course we don't,' Shona assured him. 'Just get a move on!'

'Two minutes!' Aaron called over his shoulder as he let himself out of the room. 'See you in there.'

I couldn't help feeling a tiny flicker of worry. Had I done the right thing bringing them both? I didn't want to spend the whole week feeling torn between the two of them.

I went back inside to change. I'd bought a new swimming costume for the holiday, so once I turned into a mermaid in the water, my top half would be as sparkly as my tail.

Coming back outside, I slid off the balcony and

joined Shona in the water. It folded around me like warm caramel, and I instantly stopped worrying about anything else.

My toes went numb, then my feet. Then my legs stiffened up. Finally, they disappeared altogether. In their place, a purple and green tail splashed on the surface of the water, sprinkling a rainbow arc of droplets around me.

As I dived under the surface, I got that feeling it gave me every single time.

I was home.

The three of us sliced through the water together, exploring the rocky caves below us and darting through skinny tunnels. We swam to the surface and floated on our backs as we gazed at the beauty surrounding us.

'Which d'you reckon is bluer?' I asked. 'The ocean or the sky?'

'Ocean,' Aaron replied.

'Sky,' Shona said at the same moment.

I laughed. 'They're both stunning, either way,' I said. Then I flipped over and dived down under the surface again.

Even the sea life here seemed particularly serene

and beautiful. A small group of thin fish with pastel pink blobs on their bodies and yellow markings round their eyes like make-up drifted by with the slightest flick of their tails.

A bright purple fish with a white stripe across its back and a big, black, open mouth glided alongside us. Reeds waved so gently below us it was as if time had slowed them down.

It was perfect. Every bit of it. And as the three of us swam and played and explored the day away, I knew that we wouldn't have a single worry all week.

I woke to the sound of water lapping gently against the decking outside my room. It was the second day of the holiday and we'd agreed to meet on Mum and Millie's balcony for breakfast. All the hotel's meals were self-service and they had said we could take our food and eat together in their room.

I chose some cereal and fruit from the dining room, and grabbed a drink and some bits and pieces off the deli counter to take to Mum and Millie's room.

'Tea?' Millie asked as I joined the others on the

balcony. She was opening a zip-lock bag full of teabags as the kettle came to the boil. 'Brought my own,' she explained. 'I couldn't go a whole week without my Earl Grey.'

'I'm fine with my orange juice, thanks,' I said as I pulled out a chair.

'Right, we're all here,' Mum said, getting up and nipping inside. 'Look what I've got.'

She came back out with an armful of leaflets. Spreading half of them across the table, she handed the other half to Dad to share with Shona. They were both perched on the balcony, their tails dangling over the side into the water.

Aaron and I looked through the leaflets on the table. There were boat trips, island tours, nature walks – all sorts of activities. 'We could do a different thing every day,' I murmured.

'Not sure how Shona and I would get on with the Pitch and Putt,' Dad said, laughing.

I picked up a leaflet. '"The Falls of Forgotten Island,"' I read from the front page. It had a picture of a small island with a mountain in the middle of it, stretching way up into the sky. A massive, white, frothing waterfall crashed all the way down the side of the island.

The picture showed a bright yellow boat in a still stretch of water at the base of the waterfall. Along the bottom of the leaflet, in bright yellow letters that matched the boat, it said: 'Visit the recently discovered Forgotten Island and its magical waterfall. Daily trips with Majesty Tours throughout the year.'

I held the leaflet out to Mum. 'That looks pretty awesome.'

Mum glanced across at it. 'Gosh. Doesn't it!'

Millie plonked herself down next to Mum and looked over her shoulder. 'Oooh,' she said with a loud slurp of her tea. 'Count me in for that one.'

'How about you guys go on the boat trip?' Dad suggested. 'I could take Shona on a species-spotting trip along the seabed?'

I caught Shona's eye. She didn't look thrilled at the idea, and I didn't want her to feel left out, especially on the first day.

'I won't go,' I said.

Shona frowned. 'You have to go. It looks totally swishy.'

I thought for a moment. 'Come with us!' I said.

Millie flipped the leaflet over. 'Um, Emily,' she said carefully. 'You know it's all on a boat, don't you?'

I grinned at Shona. 'You could swim along beside the boat. It'll be fun.'

'You sure it wouldn't be dangerous?' Mum asked. 'We're responsible for Shona while we're away.'

'I guess I could come at least part of the way,'

Shona said. 'Maybe not all the way to the falls, but I could head out towards the island. Far enough to feel like I'm with you. Kind of.'

'Not "kind of" at all,' I assured her. 'You'll *totally* be with us.'

'All right.' Dad gave in. 'But be careful.'

'Of course,' Shona agreed.

Dad turned to Aaron. 'What about you, young man?' he asked. 'Boat or seabed trail?'

Aaron took a bite of his toast. 'Um. I'll go on the boat, please,' he said. Holding my hand under the table, he added more quietly, 'That way, we get to spend the whole day together.'

And yes, of course that made me feel nice. And yes, it was what I wanted too. But I was desperate to make sure Shona didn't feel left out, so I shovelled a spoonful of cereal into my mouth and mumbled, 'Yeah, cool, whatever,' as casually as I could.

As Mum went inside to call reception and book the trip, I pushed my chair away and went to sit on the decking next to Shona.

Shona smiled and shuffled over to make space. It wasn't her usual smile, though. Her mouth made a smile shape but her eyes didn't.

'You OK?' I asked.

'Yeah, course,' she said in a flat voice.

'Hey. What's up?'

'Nothing, honestly.'

I raised an eyebrow.

'OK, then.' Shona waved the leaflets at me. 'Just, I dunno. All this,' she said. 'It's all stuff I can't do in the same way as you. I don't want to hold you back from enjoying your holiday. '

I laughed. 'Shona, you're my best friend. You could never do that!'

Shona pulled a face. 'I know. I'm being silly. Sorry. I guess I thought we'd just be hanging out, not going off on excursions. You, me and Aaron, doing nothing. Like we agreed.' She gave me a pointed look. 'To be honest, I don't know if swimming across the bay to a forgotten island on my own and watching you guys enjoying yourselves on the boat is going to be all that much fun for me.'

Shona was right. We were meant to be chilling out, or swilling out, or whatever. We'd agreed, and I didn't want to let her down. I was about to say I wouldn't go on the trip. We'd hang out doing nothing together all day. And then Mum came back outside.

'Right, that's all booked,' she said. 'We meet on Paradise Quay at two-thirty.'

I turned to Shona.

'Look, you go on the trip,' she said. 'I'll stay around here, or go on the seabed trail with your dad. It's only going to be for a couple of hours.'

'Are you sure?' I asked.

She nodded.

'I promise I'll just go on this one trip, OK? Then we'll spend the rest of the week doing nothing except soaking up the sun and the sea together.'

Shona smiled, and this time it reached her eyes. 'Only if you want to.'

'Course I want to. One excursion, then it's swishy swill time. No mysteries, no crazy adventures. No breaking our deal.'

Shona laughed. 'Sounds good,' she agreed.

I grinned and gave her a big hug. Droplets of water sparkled around us as our tails flickered with excitement. Today was going to be *swishy*!

CHAPTER 3

'Ladies and gentlemen, please listen to the following safety announcement. You may move freely about the boat on our journey to Forgotten Island, but you must remain within the white lines around the edge of the deck at all times. Where possible, please hold on to the rails. We will drive as close as possible to Forgotten Island. This means that those of you who wish to view the waterfall from the deck WILL get wet. We are here for your enjoyment, but your safety is paramount and we must remind you that it is NOT safe to go beyond the white lines. Thank you for listening and we hope you all have a magical trip with us today.'

We pulled on the waterproofs they'd given us. They looked like enormous yellow tents.

'I quite like this,' Millie said, looking down at herself. To be fair, it wasn't that different from the flowing capes she wore most of the time. 'Might have to see if they'll let me keep it.'

'Where do we want to sit?' Mum asked.

'The front!' Aaron and I said in unison.

Mum frowned. 'I don't know. It could be very slippery if it gets wet. You heard the announcement.'

Millie made for the door that led into the cabin. 'Do what you like, kids. I'll be keeping warm and dry. Laters!'

'Think I'm going inside with Millie,' Mum said. 'Promise you'll be careful, and do what the man said. Keep hold of the rails, and stay inside the lines.'

'We will,' I assured her.

'I'll look after her,' Aaron said as he put an arm around my shoulder.

I raised an eyebrow.

Aaron laughed. 'On second thoughts, it's probably more likely to be the other way round,' he added.

I laughed back.

'I mean it. Be careful, OK?' Mum insisted.

'Mum, we will.'

'I'm going to go and join Millie, then. See you later.'

Aaron took my hand and we made our way to the front deck. There were a few people there already: a young couple taking photos of each other; an elderly man pulling on his yellow waterproofs, and a family with two children packed in tightly between Mum and Dad.

'Here.' Aaron pointed to a space in the middle of the deck. We squeezed in and waited for the boat to start moving.

The engine suddenly revved loudly and one of the crew members jumped aboard with a rope. 'Anchors aweigh!' he shouted. 'We're off.'

After that, the engine settled into a regular *putt putt* sound as we left the dock and started sailing out into the bay. We couldn't see Forgotten Island yet, and I leaned on the railing and looked around as we glided along.

The sparkling blue sea deepened as we chugged out of the bay, with a clear blue sky to match it.

The engines grew louder and the water grew darker as we left the bay behind and sped up. Soon, I could see something ahead of us. It was still a speck in the distance, but as we grew closer I recognised it from the leaflet. Forgotten Island.

All around the island, harsh, jagged cliffs rose directly from the sea, shooting upwards like giant rockets. The one at the front looked white, as if it were made from chalk. A mountain top towered behind the cliffs.

A ring of cloud encased the whole middle section of the island, the peak of the mountain poking out above it.

As we approached, I realised that the white cliff wasn't a cliff at all. It was the waterfall. Cascading down from the top of the island and crashing into the sea below, it was the biggest, angriest looking thing I'd ever seen in my life. More powerful, even, than the Great Mermer Reef that protects Neptune's prison.

'Aaron,' I whispered, clutching his arm.

'I know,' he whispered back.

The boat chugged slowly towards the island. As we drew nearer to the falls, I stopped being aware of anything else. Even the boat and my fellow passengers. Even Aaron.

Closer, closer. Bit by bit we edged forwards. The nearer we got, the more I could see. The cloud shrouding the island hovered like a belt around its middle, flashing different colours as the spray from the falls shone rainbows through it.

My eyes watered from the spray, but I still couldn't tear them away. All I could do was stare and stare.

Aaron pulled me close. 'Mind-blowing, isn't it.'

'Totally.'

The boat was now directly facing the falls and

still edging closer. Ahead of us, the enormous cliff side was coated in an icing of white, frothing water that pounded ferociously over rocks, hitting them so hard the spray rose almost as high as the cliff itself.

The base of the cliff was like a wide skirt: an arc of land that jutted out like a stage. From there, the cliff rose in jagged sections – each one set back a bit further than the one below it, narrowing gradually the higher up it went. I couldn't see the top of it.

The boat's engine revved as furiously as the roar of the waterfall.

Around me, I was vaguely aware of people taking photos, calling to each other. But the voices faded more and more as we drove further and further into the spray, edging ever closer to the falls themselves.

I closed my eyes and felt the water on my face. Spray kissed my cheeks, fluttered on my eyelids. The screaming of the boat's engine was swallowed up by the thunder of the falls.

I had never felt this way before. So engulfed by a place and so entranced by a beauty that I could not only see, but feel and taste and hear. Every sense was alive to the moment, and I never wanted it to end.

Unfortunately it was about to, as a voice crackled over the speaker.

'Please could I have your attention, ladies and gentlemen. We will soon be driving as close as it is possible to get to the falls without endangering lives. As well as the turbulence from the waterfall, this part of the ocean suffers from high swells and unpredictable tides. In order to guarantee your safety, we are now asking that all passengers come inside the boat. I repeat, will all passengers now come inside the boat. Thank you.'

I looked around us. Almost everyone else had gone inside already. Even with the yellow macs we'd been given, we were getting a drenching out here. Most people didn't need an announcement to make them go indoors.

There was only Aaron and me, and a young couple at the far end of the deck. They were huddled together like us, but facing away from the island. Arms tightly wrapped round each other, macs pulled over their heads, one of them held an arm out to take a selfie with the falls behind them.

'Hey, we should take one too,' Aaron said.

'I haven't got my phone.'

Aaron laughed. 'Me neither.' He pointed at the couple who had now finished taking their photos and were carefully starting to make their way inside. 'I guess we should go in.'

I sighed. 'I suppose.'

But as we turned, I spotted something in the sea. 'Aaron!' I grabbed his arm. 'Look!' I pointed down at the water, but it had gone, replaced by thundering waves and froth from the falls.

'I can't see anything,' Aaron replied. 'What was it?'

'I don't know. A big fish of some sort I reckon. Maybe a seal, or a small shark?'

'Or just a rock,' Aaron replied.

'Yeah, probably,' I agreed. My imagination working overtime as usual.

As we made our way towards the door, I saw it again: a shadow under the water. 'Aaron!' I jabbed a finger at the water. 'It's there again! And it's definitely moving!'

Aaron squinted into the water. 'Yes, I see it!' he said. 'Looks like it's coming towards the boat.'

'Let's check it out,' I said. We were approaching the door that led inside, but further along the deck, a small set of steps at the back of the boat led down to a lower deck.

I glanced round. We were the only ones still out here now. 'We could probably get down there without anyone knowing,' I said.

'Em, I don't think we should. The man—'

'I know,' I said. I hesitated for a second as my deal with Shona flashed into my mind. Was this breaking it?

No. I didn't think so. I wasn't going off looking for a mystery. I just wanted to see what was in the sea beside us.

'Just a quick look,' I urged. 'And then we'll go in.'

'OK, but be careful, all right? It's dangerous out here.'

'We're semi-mers!' I said with a laugh. 'What's the worst thing that can happen? We'll fall in the water. Big deal!'

Aaron half sighed, half laughed. 'Oh, all right then,' he relented. 'I know you'll have to do it now the idea is in your head, and I'm not having you go alone.'

I led the way to the top of the steps. With a quick look round to make sure no one was watching us, we climbed over the 'Staff Only' sign and, gripping the rail all the way, stepped carefully down to the lower deck.

'It's a bit different down here!' Aaron yelled as we clasped the railing and braced ourselves against the spray as the boat thrashed heavily from side to side. The force of the falls felt even stronger on this deck as we were so much closer to the water. It felt almost as if we were driving right into the falls. It was like being in the middle of a misty downpour.

'It's wild, isn't it!' I yelled back.

Aaron's face was paler than usual. It was actually starting to look a bit green. I guessed being a semi-mer wasn't necessarily protection against the effects of being hurled around on the lower deck of a boat. Even *I* felt a tiny bit nauseous and I'd lived on a boat all my life!

I looked into the water. All I could see was white froth now. No sign of the seal or shark or whatever it was.

I turned back to the waterfall as the engine screamed to hold our position.

It felt as if we were in a whole new world, driving further and further into the mist.

I stared hard into the frothing white water, almost willing myself to become part of it.

As I stared, I saw something. Not in the water. Behind the falls.

Surely it couldn't be – could it?

I wiped my eyes and pulled my hair off my face. Then I stared even harder.

One section of the falls seemed to flow a tiny bit less fiercely than the rest. I could just about see the dark of the rock behind it. And for a brief moment – only a couple of seconds – I saw something else. A flash of colour behind the falls; a splodge of something green against the dark rock.

At first, I assumed it was a tree.

Then I saw something else.

I glanced at Aaron. He was clutching on to the railing and had his head down.

'Aaron.'

He looked up. 'Huh?'

'Did you see that?'

'See what?' He was definitely green now. He looked like he was about to be very ill.

'Doesn't matter,' I said. 'Come on. Let's go back up.'

I turned back to the waterfall for one last look as we made our way to the steps. Yes. It was definitely there. I wasn't imagining it.

There, among the rocks, behind the thundering falls that surely no human could survive. Right there, I was sure of it.

I saw a person. I saw a face. I saw a pair of dark eyes, boring through the falls and the mist and the frothing, rushing water, and connecting with mine.

CHAPTER 4

'There you are!' Mum was by my side within seconds of us sneaking inside. 'I've been looking for you. This is fun, isn't it?'

'It's swishy!'

'I'm just going to sit down,' Aaron said, and stumbled to the chairs at the back of the cabin.

I spotted a man in a Majesty Tours uniform on the other side of the cabin. 'Back in a sec,' I said to Mum, and before she could ask where I was going, I was across the room and waiting for the man to finish the conversation he was having on his walkie-talkie.

39

He ended his call and was about to move off when I touched his arm. 'Excuse me.'

He glanced down at me and gave me a smile. 'Yes, young lady. How can I help you?' he asked.

I tried to figure out how to put my question into words.

'I, um. Do you, errr . . .'

The man looked at his watch. 'Sorry, miss, I haven't got time for—'

'Has anyone ever been seen in the falls?' I blurted out.

'Has anyone what?'

'Has anyone – I mean, like, is it possible that someone could swim behind the falls and, well, kind of . . . hang out . . . there . . . ?'

My words fell away from me and my faced burned. What an idiot. I sounded ridiculous. The man obviously thought so too. He burst out laughing.

'Ha ha, you kids have such great imaginations,' he said. Then he leaned right down, as though bending to talk to a little kid. 'It's a fun idea,' he said. 'You should ask your mummy if you can go home and write a story about it.'

I bit my lip. My face burned even hotter, this time with irritation.

The man straightened up again. 'Look, we haven't been running these trips for very long. You know why?'

I shook my head.

He lowered his voice and said, 'Because no one knew this island existed till last year.'

'Seriously? How come?'

'It was completely hidden behind clouds,' he said. 'Clouds that never went away. All this time, we never knew there was an island here. It got left behind the rest of the world.'

'Which is why it's called Forgotten Island?' I asked.

'Exactly.'

'So why did they clear? What changed?'

The man shrugged. 'I guess something in the air, or on the seabed. Out here, any small change in nature causes something else to alter. We don't know what it was – but we're not complaining.' He jabbed a thumb in the direction of the falls. 'Are you?'

'Not at all,' I replied.

'And to answer your question, no, it's absolutely impossible,' he went on. 'There is no one living there. No one can even *get* there. Between the dangerous swells on one side, the treacherous falls on the other and cliffs like monstrous spears in between, I can assure you that there is *no* possibility of getting behind the falls and hanging out there. Does that answer your question?'

I gritted my teeth. 'I guess so,' I mumbled.

'Good.' The man smiled a smarmy I-know-so-much-better-than-you kind of smile and went on. 'Do you know how much water comes hurtling down that mountain?' he asked.

I shook my head.

'Almost two hundred thousand cubic metres *every minute.*' He leaned back and folded his arms across his chest.

If I'm honest, I didn't really understand exactly what that meant – but it sounded like a lot. So I gave him the answer I thought would make him happy.

'Wow,' I said.

'Uh huh,' he replied, looking so smug you'd think he'd actually built the waterfall himself.

'So, I guess that makes it hard for someone to swim through it?' I asked.

The man laughed again. 'Hard?' Then he beckoned me over to the window. I followed him and looked out to the mass of white spray as he pointed. 'You think it's *hard* to swim through that?' he asked.

Before I could answer, he went on. 'It's not hard. It's *impossible.*'

'Has anyone ever tried?' I insisted.

He frowned. 'Actually, yes. When it was first discovered last year. A young man tried.' He shook his head. 'Such a sad case.'

'What happened?'

He held my eyes for a moment before replying

42

in a low voice. 'He was never seen again.'

'He . . .'

He nodded. 'He died.'

I gulped.

'So, no. It is not possible. Anything else?'

I shook my head. 'No. Thanks.'

And with a sharp nod, the man walked off and left me standing in the window, looking out at the avalanche of white, frothing water.

'Ladies and gentlemen, we shall soon be moving away from the falls. As we leave Forgotten Island, you may return to the outer deck. Please be aware that we can experience moments of turbulence at any time, so always remember to hold on to the rails. Your safety is our paramount concern. After we leave, we shall be taking you on a tour of the area and are due to return to the dock on Majesty Island in approximately two hours.'

Mum and Millie were sitting together, looking out of the window; Aaron was still at the back. I went over to join him.

'Want to come back outside?' I asked him.

Aaron groaned. 'I'm not feeling too great,'

he said. 'Must have eaten something a bit off at breakfast. I'll be OK soon, I'm sure. You go out. I'll join you in a bit.'

'I'll stay with you,' I said.

'No! Don't miss out. Go. I'll come find you as soon as I feel a bit better.'

I got up from my seat. 'As long as you're sure?'

'Of course I am.' Aaron gave me a weak smile.

'All right. See you in a bit,' I said.

Now we'd been given the all-clear, at least half the passengers were making their way outside. I went to the front deck where we'd been earlier, but it was packed. Even the sides of the boat had people squeezed into every bit of space.

I was desperate for one last look at the falls, so I picked my way along the deck and approached the stairs at the back of the boat.

That was when I saw it again. The shadow in the water. This time it had come closer to the boat. Close enough that I could see what it was. Or rather, *who* it was.

'Shona!' I yelled. She must have changed her mind and decided to join us after all! She was under the water and hadn't seen me yet.

I glanced round the boat. No one was looking this way. Right. That was it. I was going down there again. I wanted to see Shona — and, yes, if I'm honest, I wanted to feel closer to the falls again. Just one last time.

With one final look round to check no one was watching, I slipped to the back of the boat, hopped over the barrier and carefully slipped down to the lower deck.

Gripping the rail so hard my hands were white, I inched along the deck.

Luckily, the upper deck extended further out than the lower one, so no one would be able to see me from above.

Craning my neck to look into the water, I searched for Shona.

Where was she?

I clung to the railing and stared harder.

And then I saw her.

'Emily!'

'Shona!' I yelled, leaning over the railing. She was close to the boat, her head bobbing above the water. 'You came!' I called down.

'I thought I'd surprise you!' Shona called back. 'Didn't want to miss out on seeing the falls!'

'They're stunning, aren't they!' I shouted down to her.

'They're the swishiest thing ever!' Shona yelled. She was treading water with her tail, but kept bobbing under. The swell was strong, and so was the force from the falls.

'You OK there?' I called the next time her head bobbed above the water.

'It's really hard to keep my head above the water,' she replied. 'I think I'm going to head back. See you at the hotel.'

'Wait!' I shouted. I'd had a thought. The boat had fully turned away now, and I was at the back, facing the falls. My last chance to see if I'd been right about seeing something. Maybe Shona had seen it too.

'What is it?' she called up.

'I thought I saw something! In the falls.'

'Saw something?'

'Yeah.' I stared across at the white froth thundering down over rocks. Mouth open, I gazed at the rainbow rising above the spray, like a bridge into the beauty. For a moment, it took my breath away. The mist on my face felt like snowflakes on my cheeks.

'What kind of something?' Shona called.

'I . . . I'm not sure. Like, maybe a person.' I stared into the falls, trying to find the spot where I'd seen the eyes, already convincing myself I'd imagined it.

The man had been right. Of course he had; he knew what he was talking about. I'd imagined it. Just a flicker of light, colours bouncing against the flow of water. I was a fool.

As I stared, a sudden wave hit us side-on, making the boat dip heavily to one side, then rock back the other way. Up on the passenger deck, they were fine, but down here, the spray from the swell shot across the deck, almost knocking me over. I gripped the railing.

Another wave hit the boat. A sudden lurch and—

Wait! What was that? Was it . . .

I knew I should go back upstairs where it was safe, but I couldn't tear my eyes away. This was probably my last chance, and I was *sure* I'd seen it again. Was it a face?

'Shona! There! Look!'

'I can't see anything!'

Leaning across the railing to get closer, I reached up to wipe the spray out of my eyes. In that moment, I saw it again.

'There!' I yelled, and with my other hand, I pointed and jabbed at the falls.

In the same second, the boat took another sudden lurch, dipping down hard at the back.

My feet slipped. I didn't have my hands on the railing. I was on the floor.

'Emily!' Shona screamed from the water.

I didn't have time to reply. Didn't have time to think about what to do. Didn't have time to grab the railings. Didn't have time to do anything.

With one more lurch, the boat dipped forwards,

then sharply back again, and I slipped off the deck and into the water.

What was happening? Where was I? Where was the boat?

My thoughts tumbled and thrashed around in my head as my body tumbled and thrashed around in the water.

What had I done?

Why had I been so determined to get Shona to see what I saw, when it was probably – definitely – just a trick of the light?

Where *was* Shona?

Kicking frantically with my legs, I tried to swim back to the surface, but the weight of the water kept pulling me back down.

I wanted to cry, but even that felt pointless. My tears would be nothing compared to the gushing from the falls.

And then a familiar feeling gave me at least a tiny bit of comfort.

My legs melted away, and in their place, my tail formed.

OK. I was a mermaid now. I could relax.

'Emily!'

Shona was in front of me. I swam to her.

'What happened?' she asked.

'I fell in!'

'I know, but how come?'

I paused. I didn't want to sound stupid. I didn't want Shona to laugh at me.

'What is it, Em?' she pushed. 'You can tell me anything.'

She was right. Of course she was. She was my best friend!

'Well, I kind of saw something,' I began. 'Behind the waterfall.'

'The island, you mean?'

I shook my head. '*On* the island. I thought I saw a pair of eyes.'

Shona stared at me. Before she had a chance to say anything, I had an idea. 'Let's go and check it out!' I said. 'Just swim as close as we can get to the falls, poke our heads up and see if we can see them again. It'll take two minutes, then I'll swim back to the boat.'

Shona frowned. 'Emily, I'm not sure. It's rough over there.'

'I know. Before my tail formed, I thought I'd never be able to cope with it. But now it has, I feel completely different. Shona, we're mermaids! It's the ocean! We'll be fine!'

'Em, what about our deal?'

I laughed. 'I know. And I promise. Two minutes.

If it starts to feel dangerous, we come straight back. No adventures, no danger. We'll just swim as close as we feel safe to swim, have a quick look and come back. Just to put my mind at rest about what I saw. *Please!'*

Shona turned away from me and paused for ages. Then, with a resigned shake of her head, she turned back. 'OK,' she said. 'But two minutes.'

'Deal!'

The first minute was fine. We swam towards the falls in a current that grew strong enough to make it hard work.

It was the second minute that changed everything. We were swimming along, side by side. I turned to Shona and gave her a thumbs-up. 'I told you it would be—'

I didn't get to finish my sentence. A massive rush of water ploughed into me like a medicine ball, snatching me up and spinning me round. It felt as though I'd swum slap bang into the middle of a ferocious whirlpool.

'Emily! Are you OK?'

I could hear Shona calling to me, but I couldn't see her. All I could see was white, frothing water all around me. I couldn't get past it.

'Shona!' I called back, starting to panic. 'Where are you?'

'I'm here!'

I peered into the haze of white, and could just

about make her out. 'OK, I'm coming,' I yelled. I tried to swim towards her, but I kept being pushed back down.

'Grab my hand!' Shona called. She was trying to swim to me.

I reached out for her. She was so near. 'I can't – can't reach you,' I gasped.

As the water swirled around me, I tried again. Shona reached for me and her arm made it through the swirling water. Finally, we managed to clasp hands.

'Hold on,' Shona said. I gripped her hand as water streamed past us, lifting us, shaking us, pummelling us and spinning us round and round, inside out.

I remembered the story the man on the boat had told me, about the young man who'd died.

Could *we* survive this?

'Emily! We have to get out of here!' Shona screamed at me. Her face was as white as the froth surrounding us.

'I know! But *how*?'

'Keep swimming!'

'I'm trying!' I yelled.

Shona tightened her grip on my hand. 'Try harder,' she said. 'Come on, let's push together.'

So we did. We worked our free arms like windmills, thrashed our tails as hard as we could, pushed on and on.

'The current's getting stronger!' I said. 'Are we swimming the wrong way?'

'I don't know,' Shona replied. 'It feels the same in every direction. I don't know which way is up or down any more, never mind whether we're swimming towards or away from the falls.'

As the current grew stronger and stronger, I could feel the energy draining out of me. It was hopeless. We couldn't fight it.

I looked all around me, trying to work out what we could do. And that was when I noticed something.

'Shona,' I said. 'Stop fighting it. Stop trying to get through it.' I pointed to the side, where the rushing looked less frantic. 'Look, the current is slower over there. Let's try swimming sideways instead.'

Shona did what I said. Together, we swam *across* the current instead of swimming into it – and instead of being beaten backwards, we slowly started to make progress.

I couldn't see much and was so disorientated I barely knew up from down. But it was working. I still had no idea exactly where we were, but the current was slowing a tiny bit. Maybe we were heading towards the edge of the falls.

Would we make it out of here after all?

As the current slowed even more, we let go of each other and swam in single file.

Shona pointed down. 'Look,' she said. 'It's even

calmer below us. Let's head down.' She swished her tail and dived lower.

Summoning up all the strength I had, I flicked my tail, threw my body into an arc and flipped myself even further downwards. Shona was right. The lower we went, the more the bubbles began to subside.

Down, down, swishing my tail as hard as I'd ever worked it, I ploughed through the water until my body felt as if it was on fire. Shona was beside me, doing the same thing.

Finally, the current eased so much I could barely feel it. I let my tail relax.

'We've done it!' I yelled, turning to grin at Shona.

She wasn't smiling back at me.

'We'll get out of this,' I said. 'I promise.'

We looked up at the fierce rushing of water zooming past above us. I'd never seen anything like it in my life. Like the busiest, fastest motorway in the world, but instead of roads and cars, it was water, bubbles and froth.

Ahead of us, the water was still moving, but at a fraction of the speed of the mayhem above us. At least we could see through it down here. Shoals of fish dotted about, seaweed trailing, rocks poking up like mini mountain ridges.

A couple of long silver fish came towards us, swimming by without stopping or showing any interest. One was big enough that I thought for a second it might be a shark. I didn't really want to hang around.

'Come on,' I called to Shona. 'Let's swim on.'

'Which way?' Shona asked.

'I don't know,' I confessed. Down here, it all looked the same. Then something caught my eye. A tiny ray of light, like a tube. A tunnel of sunlight directly ahead of us. It looked even more still than where we were now. At least it was lighter. Maybe we'd be able to see where we were from there.

'Let's try over there,' I suggested.

Shona shrugged and followed me as we swam towards the light.

Edging into the bright, sparkly tunnel, I noticed the change straight away. No current. It almost felt as if there was no water. As though we'd hit upon some kind of vacuum: complete nothingness.

'Em, I'm not sure about this,' Shona said.

'Neither am—'

Aaaaarrrggghhhhh!

A rush of water snatched the rest of my sentence away.

Suddenly, the nothingness of the tunnel turned to absolute chaos. The calm vacuum was now a streaming, screaming tornado, lashing, crashing, hurling and whirling about in every direction.

And we were in the middle of it.

54

I'd been in whirlpools before. I'd been hurled around in the sea before. The one thing I remembered about surviving them was—

Nothing.

I actually couldn't remember *anything* about surviving whirlpools. My mind was numb and blank, and at the same time it was full. Full of water and bubbles and froth.

Plus, I had never been in a whirlpool this bad. Water threw me in every direction, spinning me round as if I was on the most sadistic theme park ride in the world.

I couldn't even see Shona any more. Was she still in here with me or had she managed to get out?

I had no idea.

So I did the only thing I could think to do.

I closed my eyes, gave myself up to the mayhem and prayed that the thunderous, rushing water would be through with me soon.

It felt as if we were in there for hours. First the heavy wash, then the spin cycle that went on for ever.

And then I realised something had changed.

I wasn't being spun round and round any more. I opened my eyes and blinked as I tried to take in where I was.

Still in the tube – but the rushing had stopped, the spin cycle was over. I could see the light sparkling again.

Despite my tail feeling like it had been tied in a hundred knots, and my arms feeling like they'd been wrung out and twisted so hard they were little more than rags, I had to recover some strength before it started again. I had to find Shona and somehow get out of here and back to the boat.

So I began to swim out of the tunnel of water. As I did, I realised that the current was on my side. The sea was growing warmer, the flow was getting stronger – and before I knew it, I was zooming along as if I was in some kind of underwater rapid.

Oh, thank goodness! I was being spat back out of the falls again.

A moment later, I heard someone beside me. 'Shona!'

She zoomed past me. 'I can't stop!' she yelled.

I swam harder to catch up with her. The water

was making it easy. The current was carrying us along.

I managed to catch up with Shona, and together we let ourselves glide.

The water felt so gentle now. Benign. We were out of the falls. I could have laughed with relief.

I smiled at Shona. 'We've done it,' I said.

Finally, she half smiled back at me. 'I reckon we have,' she agreed. 'I thought we were done for at one point.'

'Me too. I'm just glad we're out of it.'

The current was slowing. I flicked my tail to keep propelling myself along. All I had to do now was swim back to the boat, climb aboard and get back to the others, hopefully before Mum realised I had gone anywhere. Shona could swim back to the hotel and we'd meet up later and laugh about all this.

But as we reached the surface, it looked different.

'Em . . .' Shona said.

I turned to her.

'This isn't where we started,' I said. The boat was nowhere to be seen. We appeared to be in a bay of some sort. And it was kind of dark.

'Wh–where are we?' Shona stammered.

I rubbed my eyes and looked around. The land was rocky, green, lush. It wasn't like anywhere we'd been. It certainly wasn't the open ocean.

A thought was forming in my head.

It couldn't be . . . It wasn't possible. I mean, the man said . . .

As I took in our surroundings, I realised that the man had been wrong. It *was* possible. It had happened.

We'd come through to the other side. We'd survived, and now we were in a whole new world.

The world behind the falls.

CHAPTER 5

Shona and I swam towards the shore. Behind us, the rushing waterfall was a heavy white curtain closing us off from the outside world. Ahead of us, damp rocky plinths beckoned. There were no beautiful, golden, sandy beaches here.

The water lapped against the rocks so gently it was hard to believe that only moments earlier, this same water had thrashed us around so wildly we'd wondered if it would ever let us go.

'How has this happened, Em?' Shona asked as we swam.

'I – I don't know,' I confessed. 'It's not supposed to be possible. At least, it's not possible for humans.'

Were we the first to ever come here?

We'd reached the rocky shore. 'I'll climb up on to the rocks and see what's beyond them,' I said as I pulled myself out of the water and waited for my tail to melt away and my legs to re-form.

'Be quick,' Shona replied. 'I'll wait here.'

Once my legs felt strong enough to carry me, I got up and clambered over the rocks to get a better view.

I could barely see the sky. Beyond the cove, dark rocks and immensely tall trees blocked out most of the light. Here and there, breaks in the mass of green and grey allowed a few spots of sky to poke through the gaps. Sunlight sprinkled through them in tiny cylinders of light. No paths out. No signs telling us which way to go.

I made my way back down to the rocky bay. Shona was swimming around at the water's edge.

'Anything?' she asked as I approached.

I shook my head.

'What do we do now, then?' Her voice was tight, like a wire about to snap. 'Stay here and wait to be rescued? Which will never happen, as no one knows we're here and apparently it's not even possible to be.'

'We could try to get back through the falls,' I suggested.

'No way,' Shona said. 'I couldn't face that again. Not yet.'

'There might be another way out,' I said.

Shona gave me a look that told me she didn't think it was likely. Nor did I, if I was honest.

'Look, there's only one way to find out,' I said. 'Let's split up. You check out the bay; I'll go up there and see what I can find on land. Then meet back here with our findings. What d'you think?'

Shona frowned. 'I haven't got any better suggestions,' she said. 'But be quick up there. I don't want to be stranded here on my own for too long.'

'I'll be as fast as I can. See you back here as soon as one of us has found something.'

'OK.' Shona turned to swim away.

'Good luck,' I called to her.

'Yeah, you too,' she replied flatly.

I scrambled up to the back of the bay. Climbing over rocks and squeezing through overgrown leafy bushes, I carefully picked my way towards one of the shafts of light.

The rocks tapered upwards, narrowing into points, like the trees. Over the tops of them, tiny cracks let in the sky. Shards of light spread out like fans across the forest, beaming down like stars. Diamonds of sunshine danced around me, tiptoeing through the forest, waking it up.

I allowed myself a moment to take in the beauty

of it. I'd never been anywhere like this.

It was as if I was in a well; a magical, beautiful, sparkling well, hidden in the earth.

I was on the verge of feeling almost good about this place when I heard a snapping sound nearby and my heart pounded almost through my chest. I turned to look, in time to see a branch waving.

Just the wind. A breeze ruffling the edges of leaves.

As I listened, I heard more sounds. Chirping, high above me.

Birds.

What else lived here? Which animals might live in a place like this?

My feet suddenly felt like ten-ton anchors on my legs. What if there were lions, or bears, or—

Another sound! Rustling in the trees.

I ducked down, my knees on the ground, and held my breath.

Nothing. There was nothing. No one.

Of *course* there was no one. No one lived here. No one had ever been here. No one could have got in here.

I stood up carefully, slowly, and crept along the path.

What kind of creature had left this path?

I walked faster, propelling myself through the forest as if my legs could carry me away from the answers I didn't want to hear.

The ground was like a soft carpet, snaking through the trees. I stayed on the path, one step after another, head down – and then it ended. The path just stopped.

I looked up to see that it had led me to a river: a deep channel through the rocks, with what looked like a fallen tree forming a bridge across it.

I stepped towards the bridge.

Wait.

It wasn't a tree. It was tree *roots*, woven round and around each other like an elaborate plait. The bridge was adorned with stepping stones, perfectly round, evenly spaced from each other all the way along the knotted roots.

This could not have happened naturally.

A shiver ran through my body like a python slithering down my back. The sweet sounds of animals scurrying through the forest became predators spying on me from behind every tree.

What *was* this place?

I still had no answers, but I knew one thing for sure: we had to get out of here – even if it meant going back through the falls. I couldn't stay here on my own. I didn't want to explore the forest any more. I just wanted to get back to Shona and do whatever we had to do to get away from here.

I turned back the way I'd come. Hurrying along the path, I came to a fork. I was pretty sure the way back to the falls was along the left path, so after the briefest pause, I decided to take that one. I started to walk, then pace, and then – imagining hunters and monsters behind every tree – I soon found myself flat-out running.

Which was when I heard the voices.

Indecision pinned my feet to the ground. The voices sounded like they were on the other side of some trees to my right. Possibly down the other path.

Were they heading my way?

If I ran, I could probably get away before they reached me. But the faster I ran, the more noise I'd make. What if they saw me running? What if they heard me?

As I stopped moving, I stopped breathing, too. It seemed as if the whole forest had done the same.

The voices had gone. Had I imagined them?

I let out the breath that I'd been holding way too long, and was about to move when a piercing screech sounded through the forest.

What was that?

I threw myself to the ground, crouching low in the leaves and twigs. Half covering my eyes, I looked through my fingers, just in time to see a monkey swing from the branch of one tree on to the trunk of another.

I couldn't help myself. I laughed out loud. Monkeys!

That was all it had been. Of course it wasn't

people. There simply wasn't any way that people could possibly—

And then I heard another sound, and this time there was no mistaking what I heard. Human voices.

And they were heading my way.

I crawled towards the widest tree trunk and pressed myself against it. As the voices came closer, I shut my eyes, held my breath and flattened myself against the tree so hard the knobbly bark scratched my face.

Twigs snapped and leaves rustled as the people ambled by, deep in conversation.

First a low voice. A man. 'You know I will *never* do that. I will keep my faith – and so should the rest of you.' He sounded angry.

Then a reply. 'But Saul, how long will you leave it? The danger is imminent.' The other voice sounded higher pitched, female.

'What do you want me to do? Give up on the Prophecy?' the first voice replied. This time he sounded even angrier. And closer. I shrank further into the tree and tried to breathe even more quietly.

The second voice was diplomatic, bargaining. 'Of *course* that's not what I want you to do. But maybe it's time—'

'It's time when I say it is!'

Then a third voice spoke. Male again, but this one sounded younger. 'Saul, you know we're in great danger,' the new voice said. 'Not just those of us on this island. All the other islands in this ocean face danger – and all the coastlines beyond as well. Can your belief stop it from wiping us *all* out?'

The voices were coming closer all the time. When the first voice – Saul – replied, it sounded like they were right in front of me.

'That is the whole point of belief,' he growled.

'But what if it's not enough?' the female voice persisted. 'Lives are at stake here. An awful lot of lives. We have to tell people, we *have* to find a way to get out of here and warn them.'

'There *is* no way out,' Saul bellowed. 'You know that as well as I do.'

The others didn't reply. All I heard in response was the crackling of the ground as they walked away from me.

I gulped as I managed to take a few shallow breaths. What were they talking about? A threat to all the islands in the ocean? We were staying on the very next one!

I had to go back to Shona and get out of here.

The voices were a long way off now. I was pretty sure it was safe to come out of my hiding place.

I carefully slipped out from behind the tree. One step – not even one step, half a step – and then I heard it. Saul's booming voice again.

'What was that?' His voice echoed through the forest.

I held my breath and stood as still as I could, but at this point I was standing on one leg as I'd been mid-step, and I was starting to lose my balance. I gently put my other foot down, making sure to land on leaves and not tread on a twig.

'There it is again!'

That was impossible! I'd stood gently on a *leaf*! How had he heard *that*?

'Joel.' The booming voice again. 'Go see what it was. Dinner, perhaps. A bird, maybe an eagle. Go. Hurry.'

Which was when I knew I only had one option.

Run back to Shona faster than I'd ever run in my life and hope that throwing ourselves into the falls would be at least a little less life-threatening than someone hunting us for dinner.

They say fear gives you energy. Well, whoever 'they' are, they're right.

Fear, instinct and adrenaline somehow had me back at the water's edge before I could stop to think about it.

Panting and sweating, I glanced all around me

to make sure I hadn't been followed. I hadn't. The hunter must have run in the wrong direction.

'Shona!' I called, in a stage whisper that I hoped wouldn't give me away to the hunter.

Where was she?

I slipped into the water and started swimming away from the rocky shore. As I moved through the water, the familiar feeling of my legs turning into a tail calmed me a little.

Dipping below the surface, I traced the edge of the coast. I spotted her in a gap between two massive rocks.

'Shona!' I gasped, swimming over to her.

'There you are,' she said. 'I was just—'

'We haven't got time!' I interrupted her. 'Swim! As fast as you can!'

'But I thought we—'

'I'll explain on the way. We have to get out of here!'

'You found a way out?' Shona asked as we swam away from the rocks.

I shook my head as we swam. 'No. We'll have to go through the falls again.'

Shona stopped swimming. Spinning her tail to keep herself upright, she glowered at me. 'Emily, I can't go through that again.'

I took her hand, tried to pull her along. She resisted. 'Shona,' I said. 'We have no choice. There are people in the forest. I think they know we're here, and they're hunting for dinner!'

'*What?* Are you kidding me?' Shona asked.

'No. There are people living on the island, and I don't think they're happy. They sound desperate and angry. And it looks like there is a big threat coming. Shona, please, we have to get away as quickly as possible.'

Shona let out a massive sigh. Then she started swimming again.

'Thank you,' I breathed.

'Don't talk to me,' Shona snapped.

'Don't – what? Why?'

'I can't even look at you,' Shona replied frostily. 'I can't believe you've got us into this. I can't believe I let it happen.'

'Shona, please—'

'Save it, Emily. Just swim. I don't want to talk any more.'

Shona's face was set. She was really angry – and I didn't blame her. So I did what she'd said. I stretched out and flicked my tail. Reaching out with my arms, I prepared myself for the journey back.

We hadn't got far before the rushing water picked us up.

Here we go again.

I glanced at Shona. She was swimming straight into the stream of water. At first, it carried us out like a rip tide running really fast.

My hopes lifted. Maybe going back out wouldn't be so bad.

And then they plummeted again as the rip tide gathered pace and turned into a whirlpool. Before I could prepare myself or waste any more time wondering about things like whether we were going to live or die, we were hurled round and round, up, down, inside out.

My tail looped almost over my head, my arms were flung everywhere; my body felt like a ball in a particularly manic pinball machine.

I could see the same thing happening to Shona nearby.

I couldn't fight it. Couldn't beat it. All I could do was, once again, give myself up to it and let the rushing, thrashing, spinning water do its worst.

I blinked a few times as I opened my eyes.

Clear, blue water; sunlight sparkling from above. Neat groups of orange and yellow stripy fish slicing along beside me. Seaweed waving gently from a sandy seabed below me.

Had we made it? Were we through?

I swam up to the surface and wiped hair out

of my eyes. Swishing my tail to turn in a circle, I looked all around me.

Yes! We'd done it! We were back out the other side! The falls were behind us, and straight ahead I could see our boat in the distance. They hadn't got back to Majesty Island yet.

I turned to talk to Shona. 'Look, the boat is—' I began. But she wasn't there.

I ducked back down under the water and spotted her, swimming away from me.

'Shona!' I flicked my tail hard and caught her up. 'We made it!' I said, grinning.

Shona stopped swimming for a moment. 'I'll see you back at the hotel,' she said flatly, and swam off.

I wanted to swim after her, but I didn't have time. She didn't want me to, anyway. If I didn't get back to the boat before it docked, Mum would be frantic.

So I turned and swam as fast as I could.

I got to the boat just as it was coming in to the jetty. Luckily for me, that meant everyone had lined up along one side as the boat approached the dock.

I clambered up the hull on the opposite side, perching on the edge of the lower deck as my tail flickered and disappeared. Rubbing my legs, I got up and made my way round to the other side – and almost ran slap bang into Aaron.

'Emily!' He grabbed me and pulled me into a

hug that nearly crushed me. 'I've been so worried,' he whispered into my ear.

I hugged him back. It felt good. Familiar.

'What happened to you? Where have you been?'

'I'll tell you everything,' I said, drawing away. 'Where are Mum and Millie? Do they know I went missing?'

Aaron shook his head. 'I didn't want to panic them. Your mum asked where you were earlier and I said we were playing hide and seek.' Aaron grimaced. 'Is that OK?'

I smiled at him. I could hardly believe I was back here with him. I could barely believe I was back at all. 'That's perfect,' I said.

Aaron returned my smile and took my hand. 'Come on, let's get back on dry land.'

And I had to confess, that sounded like an *extremely* good idea.

We joined the others congregating in the concourse as we left the boat. When Mum saw me, all she said was how wet I was.

'We got a dunking on the deck, didn't we, Em?' Aaron jumped in before I could even think of a reply.

'Yeah, we did,' I agreed. It seemed to satisfy Mum, as she didn't ask anything else. Millie was too busy enquiring about whether she could keep her waterproof mac to even notice what we were talking about.

The four of us mooched back to the hotel together.

When we all met up for dinner that evening, I kept trying to grab a moment alone with Shona, but she wouldn't even look at me, let alone speak to me.

I had to get her on her own. I had to apologise and make it right. I couldn't bear the thought of spending the whole week like this.

I wanted to tell Aaron everything – but I had to make up with Shona first. Then I would tell them together. I needed the three of us to be a team again so we could work together to figure out what to do about the conversation I'd overheard.

The threat that was facing us all.

It was already starting to feel unreal. Everyone here was chatting, laughing, acting as though none of us had a care in the world.

Were they right? Had I heard wrongly?

This place was an utter paradise! Surely there couldn't be anything horrible going on. There couldn't be a threat.

Could there?

As soon as dinner had finished, I jumped down

from the table and perched on the decking, next to Shona.

I was planning to slip into the water and see if I could grab a few minutes alone with her. But I didn't get the chance.

Without looking at me, Shona turned pointedly to the others. 'I'm going to turn in for an early night,' she said. Then she slipped off the decking and started to swim away.

'Shona!' I called to her.

She turned to look at me for the briefest moment. Her eyes were like steel. 'Night, Emily,' she said coldly. 'I'll see you tomorrow.'

And with that, she swam off and didn't look back.

Aaron was by my side. 'Don't worry about Shona,' he said. 'She's probably just a bit upset because she couldn't come on the boat. She'll be fine in the morning, I'm sure. So, you want to tell me where you got to?'

He didn't know anything. And I was too weary to explain. I suddenly felt overwhelmed with it all. Maybe I needed to follow Shona's lead. Get an early night. Perhaps a good sleep would help me put everything straight in my head.

Whether it would solve anything or not, I knew it was what I needed.

'I'll tell you about it tomorrow, OK?' I said, and before he had a chance to answer, I added, 'I'm going to get an early night too. It's been a long day.'

I said good night to the others, then I sloped back to my room and got into bed.

I had barely hit the pillow when my eyes closed and I drifted into a hot, troubled sleep.

CHAPTER 6

'**E**mily.'
Someone was shaking me. They'd caught me!

'Don't! No! Don't take me! I'm not—'

'Emily!' They were shaking me again.

I wriggled out of their grasp. 'Leave me alone! Let me go!' I shouted.

'Emily! It's me!'

Wait, I knew that voice . . .

'It's Mum! Emily, wake up. You're having a bad dream.'

I opened my eyes and blinked in the hazy morning light. A silhouette was hovering over me. I blinked again as my breathing calmed.

'Mum,' I said.

Just a dream.

'You all right, sweet pea?' she asked.

I sat up. 'Yeah, I . . .'

'I heard you from our bedroom!'

'How did you get in?' I asked, still half asleep.

Mum pointed at the adjoining door that linked our rooms. 'Glad I did,' she said. 'You were in a terrible state. Shouting all sorts of things.'

I swallowed. 'Like what?'

'I don't even know. Most of it didn't make sense. Something about being chased and captured.'

I laughed. Or at least, I made a noise that I hoped would convince Mum I was laughing. Inside, I wasn't laughing at all.

I'd shouted stuff about being chased and captured? A sliver of doubt wriggled through me.

Had it all been a dream?

'Are you OK now, lovey?'

'Mm, yeah, sure. I'm fine, Mum. Thanks.'

Mum kissed me on the forehead and got up to leave. 'See you at ours for breakfast,' she said, and left me to get up.

As I made my way to the bathroom, the sliver of doubt followed me into the shower.

Could I *really* have dreamed it all? The world

behind the water – had it been a figment of my imagination?

Then I spotted my wet clothes hanging on the radiator and remembered being hurled around in the falls.

It was no dream.

It was real. Every terrifying, life-threatening, disaster-impending bit of it had really happened.

And it hadn't just happened to me. It had happened to Shona too. I was desperate to explain to her and Aaron about what I'd seen and heard in the forest.

I just hoped she'd stopped being cross with me.

'I'll tell you what,' Mum was saying as I joined everyone on her and Millie's balcony. 'I don't know if it's something they put in the water round here but I had the strangest dream last night.'

'Me too!' Millie agreed, slicing her roll in half and reaching for the butter. 'What was yours about?'

Mum laughed. 'We were all off on holiday. We were flying and I went to speak to the pilot. I knocked on the door, and no one answered. No one was flying the plane!'

'Oooh, scary,' Dad said. He reached up to the fruit bowl and grabbed a nectarine.

'I know,' Mum went on. 'As soon as I saw no one was flying it, we dropped right out of the sky and landed on the water. Then the plane became a cruise ship and it turned out that's what our holiday was all along.'

I laughed as I joined them at the table. Shona was sitting on the decking with Dad, her tail swishing lazily in the water. 'That's bonkers isn't it, Shona?'

Shona shrugged. 'I guess.'

'Mine was even stranger,' Millie said. 'I can't recall much of it now. I remember there was a monster in it. I think he was stealing our beach towels.'

Dad laughed. 'Those pesky holiday monsters, they always do that.'

Millie pursed her lips. 'Don't laugh, it was scary,' she insisted.

'Must be something about this place,' Mum said. 'Emily had weird dreams too, didn't you, Em?'

'Um. Yeah,' I muttered. Then I shoved a spoonful of cereal in my mouth and hoped I could leave it at that. I didn't want to tell them about waking up shouting, so they could all laugh at me. And now that Shona was clearly still giving me the cold shoulder, I didn't feel like laughing at myself either – or at anything, for that matter.

'Come on, don't leave us in suspense,' Aaron insisted. 'What did you dream?'

I finished my mouthful and put my spoon down. Aaron's insistence had given me an idea. What if I told them what had really happened yesterday, but disguised it as a dream? That way, I'd get to share it with everyone and test out their responses, so when I came to tell them for real, I could figure out the best way to go about it. Plus I could see how Shona responded, and see if she was ready to make up and talk about it yet.

'OK, I'll tell you,' I said. I took a breath, and then it came out in a big rush. My real-life dream.

'I dreamed that Shona and I swam into the waterfall we saw yesterday, and on the other side there was this land. There was a huge forest and there were animals there – birds and maybe monkeys, snakes, I don't know. And there were people living there. It was like a kind of paradise. But it couldn't have been paradise because they were arguing, and saying that thousands of people were in danger. And then one of them heard me stand on a leaf and he sent someone after me, so I ran away and jumped back into the waterfall with Shona. The water was so fierce I thought it was going to kill us. But it didn't. We swam like crazy, and eventually we both got back in one piece.'

I paused. No one was saying anything. 'And, um, and then I woke up,' I finished off.

Aaron was the first to speak. He reached across the table for my hand. 'Em, you are adorable,' he said. His eyes were dancing. He was laughing at me.

'Why?' I asked.

'Your imagination! It's just the best.'

'You're not wrong there, Aaron,' Mum agreed. She was smiling too. 'That's what your teachers have always said, isn't it, chicken?'

'Mmm,' I said, nodding sharply. I wasn't sure I trusted myself to say anything else.

'That's my girl,' Dad said proudly.

Aaron was still laughing. 'Even in your dreams, you can't resist an adventure! It's a good one, though. I love the idea of a magical world behind the falls. Don't you, Shona?'

Shona lifted a shoulder in a slow shrug. 'Whatever,' she said. 'I wasn't really listening.'

'Bet you anything we're on a ley line!' Millie declared, breaking the tension, or – more likely – oblivious to it. 'I'll look it up later. But that would account for all this.'

Mum laughed. 'Maybe you're right. My dream was so intense, it felt real.'

'Exactly. So did mine,' said Millie. 'What about you, Emily? Did yours feel real as well?'

I nodded. 'Mmm hmm.'

The conversation moved on after that. We started talking about the day's plans instead. I switched off and ate the rest of my breakfast in silence.

And so did Shona.

As soon as we'd finished eating, Shona turned tail and said she was going back to her room.

'Me too,' I said, getting up and wiping my mouth. 'I'll come with you.'

I joined her in the water and waited for my legs to transform into my tail. Shona didn't hang around, so I flicked my tail and swam hard to catch up with her.

We were swimming alongside each other in silence.

'Are you going to ignore me all week?' I asked.

Shona kept swimming.

'Shona, please talk to me.'

Finally, as we were approaching my room and her cave, she stopped swimming and turned to me.

My throat was hot. 'Please—'

'We had a deal,' Shona said quietly.

'Yes, I know. You said you didn't mind me going on the boat trip, and I promised that after that we'd—'

'I'm not talking about the boat trip,' she cut me off. 'I'm talking about the other deal. The original one.'

'The deal about doing nothing?' I asked.

Shona nodded. 'The promise we made that, for once, we would just hang out together like normal friends. The one where we swore we wouldn't get caught up in adventures. Where you wouldn't drag me into the scariest situation I've ever been in and nearly get us both killed!'

She was almost shouting. Her face was bright red.

'Shona, I just wanted to see what was behind the water,' I said. 'I thought we'd be safe – we're mermaids!'

'You *always* just want to see or do that one thing, don't you?'

'I didn't know what was going to happen!' I protested. I was glad we were under the water as tears were pressing at the edges of my eyes, and hopefully the sea would disguise them. 'I didn't think—'

'Exactly! You didn't think. You never do. You just act.'

'I'm sorry,' I mumbled.

'Look around you,' Shona went on. 'We come to the most beautiful, peaceful place and what happens? You nearly get us both killed.' She folded her arms. 'You made a promise to me and I believed you – I always do!'

My throat felt like a fire, raging so hard I could barely speak. 'Shona, please listen to me,' I croaked

83

as I reached out to touch her arm.

She shook me off. 'I *always* listen to you. We *all* do. You might have Aaron wrapped around your tail, hanging on every *adorable* word you say, but I've had enough of being dragged behind you in your wake. I'm through with it.'

'But—'

'But nothing.' Shona's voice was cold, like a rock. 'I'm done. I just want to chill out, relax, enjoy the holiday we're meant to be having. Let's just leave it like that, OK? You do your thing, I'll do mine.'

And with that, she swam away.

I waited outside her cave. I considered going in but I figured that would only make things worse.

So I turned and started swimming up to my room. As I swam, I tried to figure out how I had messed things up so badly, and if there was any way I could possibly fix any of it.

I didn't come up with an answer.

CHAPTER 7

The morning passed quite quickly, despite my gloom, and soon we were all meeting up for lunch and discussing plans for the rest of the day.

Millie waved a leaflet in the air. 'This is what I was telling you about, Mary P,' she said to Mum. Then she turned to the rest of us. 'I was chatting with someone on our trip yesterday and she told me about an excursion she'd been on with her husband a couple of days ago.'

'Which excursion?' Dad asked.

'Well, it's another boat trip to Forgotten Island, but this one goes into a cave in the cliffs beside the falls. Apparently, there are tunnels all the way into the island. Most of them are inaccessible, but you can get into this one when the tides are low enough – which they are at the moment. The boat goes into the cave and you can get out and walk along a ledge. You can't go right behind the falls but you can see behind them from the side! There's a trip going this afternoon. We could make it if we get a move on.'

As soon as Millie mentioned seeing behind the falls, my ears were on fire.

'Sounds good to me,' Aaron mused. 'What do you think, Em?'

'Give me a minute,' I replied. Then I got down from my chair and perched on the decking. 'Hey, do you want to spend the afternoon together or would you—'

'I don't care,' Shona cut me off. 'Do what you like.'

'What will you do?' I asked.

She shrugged. 'I'll be fine. Go on the trip. Enjoy yourselves.' Then she turned completely away from me; the conversation was clearly over.

No one else noticed, but Shona's reaction had made me as annoyed as she was. If she was going to be like that, there was no point trying to push her. Maybe if we went out for the afternoon, she'd have calmed down by the time we got back.

'OK,' I said to Millie. 'Count me in.'

'Me too,' Aaron said.

'Think I'll stay at the hotel with anyone who wants to do the same,' Mum said. 'I plan to spend the afternoon napping in the sunshine.'

'That sounds nice,' Shona said loudly. 'I'll stay around and *relax* in the sun with you,' she added pointedly.

'Me too,' Dad said. 'Millie, you're OK looking after Em and Aaron, aren't you?'

'Dad, we don't need looking after,' I insisted.

'I'll keep an eye on them, don't worry,' Millie assured him. 'They'll be fine.'

As we made plans to meet later, only part of me was really there. The other bit was too upset to care what we did that day. Between my best friend not speaking to me and the fact that I'd overheard a conversation saying we were all in imminent danger, it was hard to know *what* to feel.

Aaron nudged my arm. 'This is amazing, isn't it, Em?'

'Yeah,' I replied, still too upset about everything to match his enthusiasm. We were on a smaller boat than yesterday and approaching Forgotten Island from a different angle. Instead of aiming straight for the falls, we were heading for the sheer cliffs to the side of them.

We'd left Shona back at the hotel, paddling at the water's edge while Mum sunbathed on a deckchair nearby. I'd tried to make up with her one last time before we left, but she wasn't interested.

So here I was.

I stared at the falls. They were like a massive curtain, hiding half a world behind them.

Did we really swim through that?

'Ladies and gentlemen, if I could have your attention please.' A crackly voice came over the loudspeaker. 'My name is Susannah and I will be your guide today. We shall shortly be approaching the eastern cliffs of Forgotten Island. As some of you might know, this island was only discovered very recently. Due to the dangerous swells, the ferocious falls and the sheer cliffs on every side, the island itself is totally inaccessible.'

I squirmed in my seat and looked at the floor.

'At the base of the eastern cliffs, a narrow cave has been worn into the rocks,' Susannah went on. 'The cave forms the beginning of a series of tunnels under the island. It is usually completely submerged under the sea. However, on the very lowest tides, the water levels drop enough to reveal the mouth of this cave.'

Susannah paused while people gasped and nudged each other.

'Today is one of those special times when we can enter the cave in the side of the cliff,' she went on. 'As we approach, please stay well inside all the safety lines. Enjoy the trip, and if you have any questions, come and find me. I'll talk to you again once we're inside.'

The loudspeaker went off and Aaron and I joined everyone else in standing, staring ahead of us.

'Mother of goodness,' Millie exclaimed, coming up behind me as the boat edged slowly towards the cliff. 'It looks like we're about to be eaten up by a mountain!'

I turned to her and smiled. Her face was white.

'I'm going inside,' she added. 'I can't watch. You kids enjoy yourselves.' Then she threw her hood over her head, swished her cape around her neck and went back inside the boat.

Aaron took my hand and we stood together in silence. I could feel the spray from the falls on my cheek, even from here.

The temperature grew colder as we approached the rocks. The light disappeared as we slowly, carefully chugged into the dark cave in the side of the cliff.

'We have reached our destination and the engines will be stopped very shortly,' Susannah announced over the loudspeaker.

The boat had come to a standstill inside the cave. A couple of men had jumped off and were tying ropes on to a jagged plinth.

'You are free to disembark, but please take care at all times. Once we're all off the boat, I will show you the way to the back of this cave where a tunnel leads us to a viewing platform. From here you can see the falls in action. There are many more tunnels through the mountain, but most of them are inaccessible and dangerous, so please stay close. We will be leaving in thirty minutes. If anyone is keen to stay longer, you may return on the next boat if you inform me beforehand. Any questions, come and find me and I'll do my best to answer them.'

Aaron, Millie and I joined the queue of people shuffling off the boat. The captain had killed the engine and it was eerily quiet.

'Huddle round, people,' Susannah urged once we'd disembarked. 'If you would like to take advantage of my commentary, please stay close. As we get nearer to the falls, it will become very loud in here. If you prefer to do your own thing, that is absolutely fine. The tunnels go in a couple of directions from here. But whatever you do, please observe all the safety rules: do not go beyond the yellow lines, and when you are close to the edge of the rocks, always hold on to the rails. Any questions?'

No one replied.

'Right. Follow me, then.'

She started to walk along the rocky ledge and we shuffled along behind her. The group spread out a bit. Some wanted to keep up with Susannah and hear every tiny fact about the place. Millie joined them. Aaron and I hung back.

Every now and then, I could hear Susannah's voice imparting information in the distance. '. . . Rocks have been here for hundreds of years, possibly thousands . . . closest you can get to the falls . . . stalactites above you . . .'

Mostly, her voice was drowned out by the thundering of rushing water. We could hear the falls but couldn't see them. It was weird. Like being right inside them and nowhere near them, both at the same time.

The tunnel grew narrower and darker. Every now and then, a *plip* of water fell on me from above. The dark walls made me shiver.

'I'll keep you warm,' Aaron whispered, putting his arm around me. I slung an arm around his waist, while there was still enough room to walk side by side.

We turned a corner and ahead of us was a short path leading right up to the falls. It was cordoned off at the end with a bright yellow barrier, but you could actually see the rushing water beyond.

Susannah was positioned on the corner. 'Ladies and gentlemen,' she said sombrely. 'You are now standing beside the falls.'

'Wow,' Aaron breathed. 'Actually beside them. Can you believe that?'

'Mmm,' I replied.

'Can we go along there?' someone was asking.

Susannah nodded. 'Just don't go past the yellow line on the ground.'

So we made our way along the short path, waiting in line for each of the people ahead of us to take selfies with the white, frothing curtain behind them.

When it was our turn, I smiled at the camera for Aaron to take a selfie. I did my best anyway. The effort of twisting my mouth into a smile was tough. Smiling was the last thing I felt like doing.

As he put his phone away, I turned to face the water that was being hurled on to rocks below us at – what was it that man had told me? Something hundred thousand cubic metres a minute?

The sound was like being in the middle of the biggest storm you could imagine. Bigger than anything that even Neptune could create. Well, maybe Neptune *could* create it – on the worst day ever in the history of the world.

I breathed deeply, taking it in. My cheeks were

getting wet from the mist coming off the back of the spray. My ears were filled with nothing but the sound of it. I was lost again.

'Intense, isn't it?' Aaron said as we stared.

'Uh huh,' I replied.

We moved away from the edge and started making our way back to the main tunnels. Aaron reached into his pocket for something. A tiny little guidebook. 'Look, let's see where the tunnels go,' he said.

I glanced at the cover. *'Forgotten Island: Key Facts,'* I read.

'I bought it yesterday in the gift shop back at the hotel,' Aaron explained.

We moved to the side of the path and stood under one of the lights. Aaron opened his book to a chapter called 'The Tunnels of Forgotten Island'. He skipped over the first couple of pages to one that unfolded and opened right out. As he held it open, I could see it was like an old-fashioned map in dark sepia colours, full of twisting, turning paths and tunnels. It looked like a mass of roots wriggling and wiggling about under the ground.

The heading at the top read: 'An Archaeologist's Impression of the Tunnels'.

'Can I see?' I asked. Aaron handed the book over to me.

I held it out so we could read the text together.

Forgotten Island is one of the planet's true secrets. Hidden by a very thick cloud for hundreds of years, inaccessible on every side, and furnished with a waterfall of unimaginable proportions, the island is not only a mystery but a magical place.

Based on a study of the rock formations, carvings inside the tunnels and what is visible of the plant life, Artist Archaeology Inc. believe it is possible that there was once life on this hidden gem of an island. We have produced drawings of how the tunnels might once have formed walkways that led to every part of the island. Most of this is guesswork. Much of it is a leap of faith. We cannot know anything for sure. All we can do is explore and envisage what might have been.

Follow our drawings as far as you can as you explore the underground passageways, and let your imagination run wild!

'Swishy, huh?' Aaron said.

'Yeah. Very,' I replied. My mind was working overtime. Did Artist Archaeology *know* about the people behind the falls? That they were still there now? Or was this guidebook just part of the experience, a fantasy designed to make our imaginations run wild, like it said in the text?

Aaron held the map open and pointed at a straggly bit of tunnel. 'Look, I think this is the path we're on now,' he said.

He indicated up to the left. There was an alcove in the tunnel wall. 'See that recess? I reckon that was this.' He held out the map, jabbing his finger at a line that went on about ten times further than the alcove we were looking at. 'I bet this tunnel went on for miles, hundreds of years ago.'

Susannah's voice echoed through the tunnels before I had the chance to reply. 'Gather round, people.' She was shouting to be heard over the thundering water that still boomed louder than anything. We shuffled up to join the others.

'OK folks, this is as far into the tunnels as it's safe to go,' Susannah said once we'd all assembled around her. 'I hope you've all had a great time with us today. Please feel free to hang around here a bit longer if you'd like to, and do please take great care as you make your way back to the boat. If any of you are keen to stay longer, let me know and I will put you down for returning on the next boat. Once again, thanks for joining me and have a great day!'

Millie pushed through the crowd to get to us. 'You ready to head back?' she asked.

I wanted to stay behind a bit longer. Explore the tunnels some more. Feel the spray of the falls on my cheek one last time.

And I had to talk to Aaron. I couldn't put it

off any longer. I needed to tell him about what happened with me and Shona – and I was desperate to tell him about yesterday. That my dream wasn't a dream, and that there was a terrible threat coming and I had no idea what to do about it. If I didn't unload all of this soon, I felt as though I was going to burst.

'Yeah, come on, let's get back to the sea and the sunshine!' Aaron said as he shoved his book back in his pocket, and turned to follow Millie and the rest of the group back to the boat.

I pulled him back. 'Wait,' I whispered.

Aaron looked at me. 'What's up?' he asked.

'Nothing. Just – I want to stay a bit longer.'

Millie was ahead of us. She stopped and looked round. 'You coming?'

'We – um, we're going to stay around. We'll get the next boat back,' Aaron said. 'If that's OK with you.'

Millie frowned. 'I don't know,' she said. 'I'm meant to be looking after you.'

'Susannah said it would be OK,' I insisted. 'And look.' I waved my hand to show a group of people who weren't heading back to the boat either. 'There are others here. Please, Millie, put our names down for the next boat. We promise we'll be careful.'

Millie took a huge breath. 'If *anything* happens to you . . .' she murmured.

'It won't,' Aaron assured her.

Eventually, she shook her head. 'You kids,' she murmured. 'All right then. But you be careful! Promise me?'

'We promise,' Aaron and I said in unison.

'OK, then,' she said finally. 'Enjoy yourselves. See you back at the hotel.'

'Thanks, Millie. See you later,' I called.

When I turned back to Aaron, he was grinning at me like he'd just been given the best ever birthday present.

'Nice move,' he said, taking a step towards me and putting both his arms around me. 'A bit of alone time with you is *exactly* what today needed.'

I pushed him away, as gently as I could. 'No,' I said.

Aaron frowned. 'No? No, what?'

I couldn't help the irritation creeping into my voice. 'Is that all you think about?' I asked.

'Is *what* all I think about?' Aaron asked, a look on his face like a little puppy who'd had his favourite toy taken off him.

I sighed. 'I don't know. This. Kissing, cuddling and telling me I'm adorable all the time.'

'But you *are* adorable.' He reached out to tuck a strand of hair behind my ear.

'*Don't!*' I said sharply, pulling the strand back down. I didn't mean to snap. I didn't want to be horrible. And it wasn't his fault. Just, there was so much going on in my head that any second now, I knew the dam was going to break.

And unfortunately for Aaron, it looked like it was going to burst all over him.

CHAPTER 8

A aron stared at me with a hurt expression on his face.

Even that annoyed me. Couldn't he tell that I didn't want him to be soppy and touchy-feely all the time? I didn't want him to be so easily hurt. I needed him to be strong. I needed him to be the one in charge so *I* could fall apart if I had to.

Which I very much did.

'Look, I'm sorry,' I began, trying to keep my voice level. 'I just—'

'You just don't want me to be your boyfriend any more?' Aaron cut in.

'*What*? I never said that!'

'You don't need to, Emily. I can tell.'

'Aaron, why are you saying that?'

Aaron shook his head. 'Don't make me spell it out,' he muttered. 'It's obvious. You're just not being the same with me. How do you think it feels for me that you wince every time I come near you?'

'I don't,' I protested, but Aaron was on a roll, and he suddenly seemed as fed up as me.

'Or that you look embarrassed when I say nice things to you? How do you think that feels for me, Em?'

'Aaron! This isn't *about* you,' I insisted. 'It's about me.'

'Well, what a surprise *that* is!' he exclaimed, leaning back on a wall and folding his arms. 'Of *course* it's about you. *Everything's* about you, isn't it?'

I stared at him, all my feelings rolling up into a ball inside me. And then they erupted out of my mouth.

'How dare you!' I yelled at him. 'I've been wanting to tell you how upset I am about falling out with Shona. You should be there for me, not attack me when I'm down.'

'And *I've* been trying to tell *you* that I'll *always*

be there for you!' Aaron yelled back. 'But any time I get close to you, you just shrug me off. And now it turns out you only want to be with me because Shona's fed up with you.' He paused for a moment, then, scowling right into my face, he added, 'Well guess what, Emily? So am I.'

I felt as if he'd hit me in the stomach. What was going on? My two favourite people were mad at me. This was meant to be our dream holiday and it was crumbling at every edge.

Tears pricked at my eyes.

Not that I was going to let Aaron see that.

'If that's how you feel, why are you still here?' I asked, my voice as cold as the rocks around us.

'Good question,' Aaron mumbled.

'If you're so fed up with me, just go. Get on the boat. It hasn't left yet.'

'I'm not leaving you here on your own,' Aaron snapped.

'I'll tell you what, then,' I said, my anger and obstinacy getting in the way of any sensible, rational thinking. 'I'll make it easy for you. I'm off.'

And before I could even stop to think about where I was going or how I was going to get there, I turned and started walking away from him. In the opposite direction from the boat.

Aaron reached out to grab my arm. 'Emily, don't be silly. It's dark down—'

'Leave me alone, Aaron,' I said, shrugging him

off. 'Let's just go back separately, OK? You get this boat, I'll get the next one.'

'But Millie said—'

'I don't care!' I snapped. 'I need to be on my own.'

And with that, I turned and started to move away. Leaving Aaron in my wake, I walked, then paced – every footstep taking me away from all the stress, away from the upset and deeper into the darkness.

I didn't know where I was going. Even if it hadn't been dark in there, my tears were filling my eyes so much I could barely see.

How had everything gone so badly wrong?

The question played over and over again in my head as I stumbled blindly through the tunnels.

I didn't know how long I'd been wandering. I didn't know exactly which tunnels I'd gone down. I didn't know how many there actually were.

I didn't know much.

What I did know was, somewhere along the way, I had gone off the main path. There were no barriers any more. No lights. No yellow lines on the ground.

My thoughts were as murky as my surroundings.

Every time I thought about what had happened, the feeling of despair hit me again like a punch, each time harder than the last. The only way to deal with it was to stop thinking about it, and the only way to stop thinking was to keep moving.

Which meant that I was soon so deep in the tunnels I was in pitch darkness.

I stopped walking and looked around me. Tried to, anyway.

A new feeling crept up inside my body, overtaking the miserable one.

Fear.

What had I done?

My breath rasped in and out of my body in short, harsh gulps.

What if I ran out of oxygen in here?

I ran my hands along the walls. Damp. Cold.

PLIP!

Argh!

Something landed on my neck. I swatted it away with my hand.

Water. It was just a drop of water. Dripping off the end of a stalactite. I looked up. Peering into the darkness, I could just about make out the row of them above me, pointing down like arrows.

I had to calm down. I'd got out of worse than this. At least, I thought I had. I couldn't remember anything much any more.

I just knew I had to get out of here.

Focus.

I tried to recall the map Aaron and I had been looking at. Tried to stop myself from crying at the thought of how happy we'd been, and how quickly everything had gone wrong.

No.

I couldn't afford to do that. I had to think of the map. Try to visualise it, try to place myself on it now. Then figure out how to get back to the entrance.

I closed my eyes and took a few slow breaths. OK, I remembered seeing the bit with the row of stalactites, and I was pretty sure it was only a few bends away from where I'd left Aaron.

I just had to choose a direction.

I picked the one I thought I'd come down, and started gingerly feeling my way back along it.

The ceiling was growing lower. Had that happened on the way here? I couldn't remember.

Soon, the ceiling had lowered so much I had to crawl.

This felt wrong. I hadn't had to crawl on the way here.

Maybe this was a different way back?

Or maybe it was leading me further into the mountain.

I was about to shuffle round and turn back the way I'd come when something stopped me.

The sound of rushing water.

Yes! I'd found my way back. This must be a shortcut to the platform beside the falls. From there, I was sure I could find my way back to the rocks where the boat docked. So I just had to follow this track till it led me back, wait for the next boat and I'd be fine.

My spirits lifted like a helium balloon. I would get back to the hotel, find Aaron and apologise for being so horrible. Then I'd do the same with Shona. I'd do anything I had to do, to show them how much they both meant to me. I'd make it right.

And when we'd made up again, we wouldn't do anything except hang out and play and chill for the rest of the week. I wasn't going to think about doom or threats or anything. Surely I'd got all of that wrong, anyway. I must have done. This place was way too beautiful to be threatened with danger.

I was determined: we'd get the holiday back on track.

We would have the best week ever, after all.

Just as soon as I got out of here.

The sound of water was growing stronger. I crawled towards it, hand over hand, leg over leg.

Soon, the ceiling was becoming higher again, the path growing wider. I could stand.

I pulled myself up, dusted my legs down and continued along the path, my mood lifting with every step.

The noise was thundering now.

Just one last corner and I'd be out of here.

And then the last corner came – and my hopes sank back down, like a rock hurtling to the bottom of the ocean.

The sound I could hear *was* the rushing of water. But I wasn't back at the platform we'd been at with Susannah.

In front of me was a hole in the cave wall, just big enough to crawl into. At the end, this short tunnel met another, forming a kind of T-shape. But the second tunnel, set slightly lower than the first and sloping downwards, had one major difference.

This one was filled with a foaming, rushing, furious stream of water.

Now what?

I looked behind me. The obvious thing to do would be to retrace my steps. Crawl back through the tunnel and hope I could feel my way through the darkness back to where we'd started.

But when did I ever do the obvious thing?

A thought was nagging at me, pulling and

prodding at my mind, demanding I listen.

See where it leads.

I could crawl through the hole and into the tunnel. If there was rushing water inside it, surely that meant it led back to the falls. And if that was the case, perhaps it was my best way out of here. I already knew I could survive the falls, as I'd done so twice already.

I could be back at the hotel in no time.

The thought was irresistible.

So I climbed into the hole and crawled through. And then I slid into the dark, narrow tunnel and let the water whisk me away.

CHAPTER 9

*T*he water whooshed me so fast, I didn't have time to think. It took me over so completely, I transformed into my mermaid self without even noticing.

I let it carry me. I didn't resist.

Please, take me out to the ocean and let me get back to my friends.

It was all I wanted.

On and on it took me. The rocky cave around me grew tighter and smaller. Soon it was barely wider than my body. The water was thunderous.

It was as bad as being inside the falls. Worse, perhaps. It felt like a death chute; the scariest ride at a fair. And I wanted to get off.

I was beginning to wonder if I would survive it when—

Aaaaargghh!

The water gave one last kick and booted me out the end of the tunnel into a more open expanse of water.

Oh, thank you, thank goodness, thank . . .

Wait.

I swam up to the surface of the water, pulling hair off my face and rubbing my eyes. As I did, my gratitude fizzled into confusion.

The death chute of water hadn't taken me back to the falls. It had deposited me slap bang in the middle of a sparkling turquoise pool at the bottom of a well.

I twirled my tail and turned around in the water. Almost perfectly round, the pool was surrounded on every side by dark, damp rocks trailed with green moss.

I looked up. Far above me, the high walls of rock formed a jagged hole. Trees bowed over the edges, their leaves sparkling, as sharp rays of sun beamed down like a searchlight.

Where was I?

I gulped. There was only one way to find out.

I pulled myself out of the water and perched as

well as I could on a rock at the edge of the pool while I waited for my legs to come back.

Then, clinging to plants, scrunching my feet into cracks and scratching myself on jagged edges, I clambered up the rocks. My heart hammered as I climbed, but it got gradually easier. Thankfully, the rocks under my feet felt stable, and the crevices were big enough to cling to. Soon I'd reached the top and heaved myself over the edge.

I collapsed on the ground and allowed myself a minute to get my breath. And then I looked around.

Forest. Green. Lush. Silent.

My body hurt as a sob wracked through me. I hadn't found the falls. I hadn't come out into the ocean. I wasn't about to swim back to the hotel and make up with my best friends in the world.

I was, once again, stuck here all alone on Forgotten Island.

I picked myself up and started walking. Where, I had no idea. But I couldn't sit there doing nothing. Perhaps I could find the bay Shona and I had swum into yesterday and get back through the falls. It was my best hope.

It was my only hope.

I hadn't been walking for long. Maybe five minutes.

And then—

'STOP!'

The voice came from behind me. My instinct said: *run*. My feet said: *we're not going anywhere.*

So I stopped.

Footsteps behind me. Then the voice again. 'Listen carefully. I'm not going to hurt you. See those trees over there to your left? The ones with the branches entwined in an archway?'

I turned my head as far to the left as I dared. Yes. I could see them. Two thick trunks with a green canopy of leaves linking them above.

I nodded.

'Right. That's where we're going. Quick.'

Without looking behind me, I reached the trees and stepped in between them. The trunks were so close together they were almost touching. The leaves hung down on either side like curtains. It felt a bit like being in the kind of den I used to make at home when I was little. I'd get Mum to pull the chair right up to the sofa and throw a blanket over them. I'd sit under it, in between the furniture and feel safe.

I couldn't feel any further from safe now.

The voice took on a shape as my pursuer followed me through the leaves and stood in front of me.

'You!' It was the boy from yesterday. The one who'd been sent to hunt for dinner.

I swallowed hard and tried to give him my best you-don't-scare-me face, despite the fact that I was in fact very, very scared indeed.

He didn't look that old. Maybe a couple of years older than me.

He pulled his hair back and narrowed his eyes as he stared back at me. He was looking at me as if I was some kind of museum relic that he was studying.

I guess the you-don't-scare-me face wasn't fooling him, as he held up his hands, palms facing me and said, 'I didn't mean to frighten you,' in a much softer voice than he'd used so far. 'I told you, I was never going to hurt you. I just wanted to get you somewhere safe so we could talk.'

'Safe from what?'

The boy shrugged. 'Safe from all kinds of things. This is a forest,' he said simply.

I folded my arms and waited for him to go on.

'Look, I have no idea who you are or how you got here,' he said. 'But I know this. No one has *ever* got through the falls to us.' He paused and looked hard into my eyes. 'No one *can*,' he added. 'It's impossible.'

I cleared my throat. 'I know. I . . . I guess I can do things others can't,' I said.

He nodded. 'I noticed,' he said. 'Twice, it seems.

You know I saw you yesterday as well, don't you?'

'You mean when you were sent to hunt me for dinner?'

The boy laughed. 'I wasn't sent to hunt *you*. I was sent after what Saul *hoped* would be his dinner. He hadn't seen you.'

'He heard me, though, even though I barely made a sound.'

The boy shrugged. 'We are in tune with our surroundings. We can always hear an animal in the forest.'

He *couldn't* be telling the truth. They must have some kind of alarm system set up or something. I mean, it was impossible that they had heard me from that far away. *No one* had hearing like that. But then as far as he was concerned, it was impossible that *I* was here at all.

Maybe we'd both have to reconsider what we thought was and wasn't possible.

'Anyway,' he went on. 'That wasn't when I noticed you.'

'It wasn't?'

He shook his head. 'I'd already seen you. I saw you in the woods. Then running to hide behind the tree. Before we came past you.'

He saw me before I even knew they were there? How?

'I'm a watcher,' he said, as if he had read my

mind. Which, incidentally, I kind of hoped was something he *couldn't* do or he'd know how much of a lie my brave act was right now. 'My sight is better than most.'

'So you already knew I was there?'

He nodded.

'Why didn't you say anything to the others? Why didn't you give me up?'

He rubbed his chin. 'You haven't seen Saul on a bad day. And yesterday was one of them. I wasn't sure he'd take too kindly to an impossible stranger showing up in our midst.'

What was I meant to say to that? *Thank you?*

'It's not his fault. I mean, he's not a bad guy. He's just having a rough time at the moment,' the boy went on. 'We all are.'

'Why?'

He waved a hand. 'Don't worry about that. It's not your problem. Or . . . well, I suppose it is. Or it will be.' He shook his head. 'I wanted a chance to speak to you first to find out more. And now I have that chance. So . . .' He turned his dark eyes on me again.

I swallowed, and hoped he didn't notice that I'd started to tremble.

'How did you do it?' he asked in a low voice.

How was I meant to answer him? With the truth? No, I wasn't ready to give him what he was asking for. The truth was the only advantage I had over him, and I planned to hold on to that as long as I could.

'I don't have to tell you anything,' I said, trying to stop my voice wobbling.

A glint of a smile sneaked into the corners of his eyes. 'OK. Sorry. You're right.' The boy held his hands in front of him, palms up, in a mock surrender. 'Let's start again. I am Joel. Who are you?'

I paused while I considered making up a false name. But what was the point of that? Besides, my mind was so full of questions and fear I couldn't even think of one on the spot. 'Emily,' I said.

Joel smiled more broadly. He had a nice smile. His dark eyes lit up with a sparkle that softened his face. He was quite good-looking, too, now I thought about it.

What?! What was I *thinking*? I had a boyfriend! This boy had practically kidnapped me! What on earth was I doing thinking he was good-looking?

My face felt warm. 'Let's start again,' I said quickly, in an attempt to cover my embarrassment. 'I'll answer your questions. But you answer some of mine first, OK?'

'All right, Emily,' he said, smiling even more widely. 'How about this. I'll tell you about this island, about us. I'll give you our story.' He narrowed his eyes into a scowl. 'But after that, it's your turn. After that, you answer *my* questions.'

He held out his hand. 'Deal?'

I let out a breath as I considered it.

'Please?' he added. 'I promise you can trust me.'

Finally, I reached out to shake his hand. 'OK,' I agreed nervously. 'Deal.'

CHAPTER 10

'People have been on this island for many generations,' Joel began. 'No one has ever been able to find a way to leave.'

'Whoa. Really? You've never been off the island at all? None of you?'

'Not for many hundreds of years. And anything before that is the stuff of legends. We can't leave, though some have tried.'

'And . . . ?'

He shook his head. 'They didn't make it.'

'I'm sorry,' I said.

Joel shrugged. 'Our world is here. It's all we know. All my parents, grandparents, great grandparents and many generations before them knew.'

'Wow,' I breathed.

'It is what it is,' he said. 'We have developed in all sorts of ways, as each generation gives way to the next. Like any society, I suppose. Like yours.'

'How do you know about people outside of the island if you've never left?'

'We don't know much, it's true. But I watch. I see people who come to look at the falls. Like I said, that's part of my role.'

That was when something suddenly clicked. His job of watcher. His eyes . . .

'Wait. Was it you?' I murmured.

'Was what me?'

'The eyes. Through the water. It *was* – it was you, wasn't it?'

Joel nodded quickly. 'I *thought* you'd seen me – even though it has never happened before. These boats have only been coming here for the last year or so. Since the clouds lifted. Usually by the time the boat is close enough to be in range, everybody has gone inside. No one sees me.'

'How do you know that?'

Joel lifted a shoulder. 'Because they don't think I exist. So they do not question that perhaps I might. And even if they think they see something, one of the people in charge will tell them it was just a trick of the light.'

That was exactly what the man had said to me!

Joel went on. 'Sometimes I wonder if the people who run those trips know about us. They must wonder. They must question it at times. But then I suppose if they do, they will tell themselves that their imaginations are working too hard. People living on this island, trapped behind the falls – it's an impossible idea to them.'

'Joel,' I asked, 'how do you know so much about this?'

He shrugged. 'We pick things up. We may not be able to leave, but between us, we see things, we hear things, and we sense them. I've seen your boats. I've seen people holding things that they look into, talk to – machines that run your lives,' he continued. 'Here, we have stronger instincts, better knowledge of the things that *really* connect us.'

'Like nature?' I asked.

'Like nature,' he agreed. 'We hear what the earth is telling us. We see signs of activity through the tiniest gap in rushing water. We spy our next meal when it is hiding in the thickest of forests.'

'Which is how the guy you were with managed to hear me from so far away,' I mused.

'Yes.'

'That is some powerful sense of hearing.'

Joel lifted a shoulder. 'Maybe, but do you question the advances your society has made?'

I thought about the things I took for granted every day. The internet. Mobile phones. Aeroplanes. Space travel! 'I suppose there are a *lot* of amazing things out there, when you stop to think about it,' I agreed.

'Exactly,' Joel agreed. 'I just live in a different kind of reality from yours, that's all.'

He kept talking about his reality and my reality. Did he know that my particular reality wasn't the same as most people's? Had he seen me in the water? Did he know about my tail? Surely he would have mentioned it if he had.

'The trouble with *our* reality,' Joel went on, 'is that things are not good at the moment.'

I thought about what I'd heard yesterday, about the threat facing the island – and the world beyond it. The thing I'd been trying desperately to tell myself I'd got wrong. 'What's happening?' I asked.

Joel paused for a moment before replying. There was a darkness in his voice as he spoke. 'It's hard to say. We don't know every detail, but what we do know is that there's something very serious coming.' He kicked at the ground as he went on. 'We just can't agree on what to do about it.'

'What is it?'

Joel looked up. 'The ground is shaking,' he said. 'There is movement. It started a long time ago. Maybe a year, even. For months, it was very slight. A movement in the earth so slight that only the most skilled listeners noticed it. Most of us wouldn't have known about it, but for the cloud clearing.'

The cloud clearing? Wait, hadn't the man on the boat said something about that? That it could be to do with a change in nature? Had this shaking in the earth made it happen?

'It carried on like that for some months,' Joel went on. 'But in recent weeks, it has begun to intensify. It's getting stronger every day. The earth is shaking enough that most of us here can feel it.'

'What – you mean, like an earthquake? There's an earthquake coming? That's what you're saying?' My voice rose with every question.

'Yes,' he said simply. 'That is exactly what I'm saying. It threatens us all. All of us here on this island, and all of you on yours as well.' He hesitated before adding, 'When it happens, it will start a tidal wave that could threaten entire continents. It's bad,' he added, in case I hadn't figured that much out. 'Really bad.'

'But . . .' I began. I wasn't sure where to go after that. 'But . . .' I said again.

'There are no buts,' he said. 'And there is no way to stop it. Our only choice is to get away before it kills us all.'

'Are you sure? I mean, we have instruments, computers out there. Surely we'd know?'

Joel laughed drily. 'You and your machines. They don't tell you everything. You know how strong the current is in these falls?'

I tried to remember what the man had told me. Something to do with cubic metres. Hundreds of thousands. 'I know it's really strong,' I said.

'Yes. And that's the problem. The force of the falls is so great, it masks what's going on underneath the water. All your instruments are fooled by the power of the falls. They will never pick it up.'

'You're sure?'

'Unfortunately, yes, I'm positive.'

'When is it coming?' I asked, my throat as dry as the ground itself.

He shook his head. 'The one thing we don't have is a sixth sense. We cannot predict the future. But we know that the earthquake will be devastating. It could cause landslides that break off huge sections of these cliffs. Maybe even break up the entire island.'

He pointed high above us. 'Can you imagine the effect of half of this mountain landing in the sea? It would create a tsunami that could wipe out whole countries once it has travelled the length of the oceans.'

I stared at him. My heart felt as if it had stopped beating. 'So why are we here talking about this?' I asked. 'Why aren't we doing something about it? Telling people? Stopping it!'

'Like I said – we cannot get out, so we cannot warn people. And we cannot agree on how to save ourselves. There are two factions with opposing beliefs.'

'What are the beliefs?'

'My group believes we *have* to find a way to get out of here. We are not safe staying on this island, and nor are the people on the other island. We have to get everyone off the islands, and then warn the rest of the world.'

'So what's stopping you from trying to do this?' I asked.

'Other than the fact that there is no way out?'

'Yeah,' I conceded. 'Other than that.'

'In a word? Saul.'

'The guy you were with yesterday?'

'Yes. Saul is our leader, and we can't do anything without his say-so. His faction doesn't believe we should take action yet.'

'What do they believe?'

Joel looked down. Scuffing the ground with his feet, he shook his head and mumbled his reply. 'They believe in the Prophecy.'

'The *Prophecy*? What is that?'

Joel bent down and picked up a stone from the ground. 'See this?' he asked, passing it to me. 'To me, it's a stone. That's it, just a stone. To Saul and his followers, it's more than that.'

I studied the stone. 'More than a stone?' I asked.

'Well, not this one. But others like it,' he said. 'Some of the trees, some of the rocks – they have drawings on them. To my group, these are no more than etchings drawn by people long dead, idling away the hours on a lazy day. Sometimes they just look like random patterns.'

'And to Saul?'

Joel laughed wryly. 'A couple of times, there have been things in the drawings that have happened in our real lives.'

'What d'you mean? Like what?'

Joel sighed. 'In the west forest, there's a big rock with something etched on it that looks like a rainbow. Next to the rainbow is something that looks like rocks sliding down a cliff.'

'And . . . ?'

'And one day a couple of years ago, there was heavy rain followed by brilliant sunlight. A beautiful rainbow lit up the sky. The rain had destabilised the hillside. The ground was loose, and a few rocks slid down the hill.'

'Like in the picture?'

'Exactly. But it was a coincidence. I mean, a huge downpour like that leading to a loosening of the soil – that's nature. That's science. It's not a prophecy.'

'So there have been more events like that?'

'Yeah, one or two other things happened that bore a tiny resemblance to something from the ancient etchings. When the third one happened – a tree falling into the river and being washed away – Saul decreed that from that point onwards the etchings were to be regarded as a prophecy. If anyone found one, it was to be brought to him. He started collecting them, studying them.'

'Wow. And your faction doesn't think they mean anything?'

Joel shook his head. 'Sometimes I wish I *did*. But I don't. I believe in reality, in nature, in science, in things I can see in front of my eyes.'

I couldn't help smiling to myself. Joel sounded like Aaron. I wondered briefly if they would ever meet. The idea made me feel weird, but I wasn't sure why.

'But Saul – he won't do anything unless a drawing shows it,' Joel went on. 'Unless one of his pictures points the way, he's not going. He even wears one around his neck – a stone with a picture he believes will save us all.'

'And you think that while you sit around waiting to be saved, it's going to be too late and the earthquake will come along and wipe us all out?'

'That's it exactly,' Joel agreed.

'And he won't listen? Even to you? You looked pretty friendly yesterday.'

'Oh, we are close, in some ways. He relies on me for my hunting skills. He keeps me near when he needs me. He's been like an uncle to me most of my life. He and my father were best friends.'

'Were . . . ?'

'Before they fell out over all of this. My father is the leader of my group. He and Saul no longer speak.'

'What a mess,' I murmured.

'Exactly.' Joel looked round then moved his head closer to me. 'But maybe you can help me change his mind.'

'Me?' I gasped. 'What have I got to do with it? What makes you think he'll listen to *me*?'

'In all of these hundreds of years we've been here, the one thing we have never managed to do is find a way off the island. The only way out is either through the falls, which we cannot attempt without risking death, or through Blue Pool, which leads to life-threatening underwater tunnels with powerful currents. It's impossible. Or at least, we thought it was. But you've shown that it can be done. If you speak to Saul, he won't be able to ignore our argument any longer. He will see that it is possible to cross the falls. We can tell him how you did it – and perhaps then he will finally agree to stop believing in magic and nonsense, and listen to reason. And then we can all get out of here and off this island before it's too late.'

Joel spoke so fiercely, it was hard not to get caught up in his argument. But there was one thing he was missing; one thing he didn't know. I still hadn't told him *how* I'd got through the falls. And I knew I had to. But now it felt even harder than ever. Now he'd told me he was pinning all his hopes of survival on to me, how could I turn around and tell him that he was wrong?

'So. I've told you about us,' Joel said. 'Now it's your turn. Tell me – how did you do it?'

He was right. We'd made a deal. I had to tell him. Even if it did make me feel like I was going back to the old days when I was scared of being called a freak when people found out about me.

I took a breath. 'Joel,' I began. 'Look, there's something I need to—'

I didn't get to finish my sentence. Two men and a woman were approaching the clearing. One of them called out, 'Joel, is that you? What are you up to in there?'

Joel grabbed me and shoved me into the shadows of the tree. 'Stay there,' he hissed. 'Let me deal with them.'

I ducked down in the shadows and held my breath.

'It's me,' Joel said casually, stepping out into the clearing. 'Nothing much, just relaxing, thinking, you know.'

The one who had spoken laughed. 'You?

Thinking?' he said good-naturedly. 'That's a first.'

'Ha ha, very funny,' Joel replied.

'See you later, then,' the other man said, and they started to move off.

'Wait.' The woman stopped, peering through the leaves. 'What's in there?'

'It's nothing,' Joel insisted. 'Honestly, don't worry.'

The woman squinted into the darkness as she took a few steps forward.

It was too much. I stood up, hands in the air. 'I don't mean any trouble!' I burst out, emerging from my hiding place.

The woman stepped back, looking shocked, and turned to Joel. The two men came and stood in front of me, examining me as if I'd landed in the forest from outer space.

I guess to them I might as well have done.

'I can explain,' I said in a tiny voice.

'I think perhaps you're going to have to,' one of the men said. He turned to Joel. 'Unless *you* want to?'

The other guy stepped forwards and looked me right in the eyes. 'Save your explanations for our leader,' he said. He nodded towards Joel. 'You too,' he added.

Then he turned to the others. 'Let's take them to Saul,' he growled. 'He can decide what to do with them both.'

CHAPTER 11

I tried to keep my mind busy as we walked. I didn't want to think about what Saul might do to me.

Didn't want to keep remembering the moment I'd overheard him ordering Joel to hunt for dinner. I kept reminding myself Saul didn't specifically want *me* to be hunted.

The reminders didn't help all that much. I still felt like a prisoner being marched towards my doom.

'We're here,' Joel said as we arrived at a clearing

with a massive tree in the middle of it. It had the widest trunk I'd ever seen. The growly guy pointed to one side of it where there was an opening with branches criss-crossed over it. He pulled the branches away and indicated for me to go in. The others followed behind me, apart from the woman, who stopped at the door.

'I'll get Saul,' she said as the rest of us went inside.

The trunk had been completely carved out. In other circumstances, I would probably marvel at how cool it was. A little house, literally inside a tree!

In these circumstances, all I noticed was that my knees were shaking so much I wasn't sure I could keep standing much longer. What was Saul going to do to me? Put me in a cage? Lock me up? *Worse?*

I didn't have long to wait.

A deep voice at the door. 'I'll take it from here. Thanks, Maya.'

Saul.

He ducked down and came inside.

I looked up at him and tried to hold my nerve. He was tall and almost bald, with a bushy grey beard, a wrinkled face and flecked brown eyes, which were currently trained on me as fiercely as if they were daggers pinning me to the wall.

He moved silently towards me. 'What have we here?' he asked, almost in a whisper.

I tried to remember that I'd stood up to Neptune. Neptune! King of all the oceans! I tried to find the confidence I'd had back then.

But this was different. This time I was completely alone in a land that no one else knew existed. That no one else could get to except Shona – and she couldn't care less about me right now. No one but Aaron even knew I was gone.

This wasn't the time to feel confident.

'I'm s-sorry; don't kill me!' I said, as a hot tear burned the edge of my eye.

Saul flinched. '*Kill* you?' he repeated. 'Why on earth would I do that?'

'I – you – you – said – chase me . . .' I stammered.

'*What?* I've never seen you before in my life!' he boomed.

Oh no! I'd made him angry. That was the *last* thing I'd wanted to do. I swallowed hard and tried to hold my nerve. 'You – you sent Joel to chase after me for dinner,' I said, like a mouse with a particularly timid voice.

'*Chase* you? For *dinner?*' Saul sounded more bemused than angry now. 'Did you really think that?'

'I . . .' I began. What could I say? That was *exactly* what I'd thought. I suddenly felt ashamed to have got it so wrong.

'I'm sorry,' I mumbled.

Saul sighed and turned to Joel. 'Do you want to

explain what's going on here?' he asked.

Joel stepped forward. 'I found her in the eastern forest,' he said. 'I don't know who she is, how she got here or anything. I was going to bring her to you. I was planning to find out a bit more about her first.' He gestured at the others. 'They just got us here a bit faster.'

Saul turned back to me. 'So, we know nothing about you?' he asked. As he spoke, he edged closer. So close I could see the beads of sweat on the top of his head.

So close that I could see his necklace.

The one that Joel told me about. What had he said? That the necklace had a picture of the thing Saul believed was going to save them all.

As I looked at the pebble hanging round Saul's neck, I couldn't help gasping. I clapped a hand over my mouth. *No.* It couldn't be. It *couldn't*!

'What's wrong?' Saul asked, stepping back. 'I'm not going to hurt you.'

I couldn't speak. Couldn't find words. All I could do was hold out a quivering arm, stretch out my hand and point at his necklace.

The picture on the pebble – it was a person. Kind of.

It was a girl with shortish hair. She was waving as she swam in a lake.

And she had a mermaid's tail.

My stomach turned right over as my eyes confirmed who I was looking at.

The person who Saul believed was going to save them all — it was me.

I tried to find my voice. It wasn't there.

'What? What is it?' Saul asked.

I cleared my throat and tried to swallow. My heart was thudding into my throat so hard I could barely breathe.

Saul turned to the men who'd brought us here. 'Fetch her some water, she looks like she's about to faint.'

The man went round the back and returned a minute later with a cup made from a coconut shell. 'Here,' he said. 'Drink.'

I sipped the water and gathered my thoughts. Tried to, anyway. They were scrambling about all over the place. The one that I kept coming back to was the fact that I couldn't exactly tell Saul I was a mermaid. I mean, it was obvious that I *wasn't* a mermaid. Where was my tail? He might have been reasonable so far, but I wouldn't like to bet on him taking kindly to what would only sound like a child's fantasies.

'Speak,' Saul said when I finished drinking. He was starting to sound impatient. 'Explain, please. Who are you? Why are you here? How did you get here?'

Everything Joel had told me was still whizzing around in my head. The earthquake that threatened us all. Actual lives were at stake. And if I was the one who could help, then I had to tell them.

In fact, I had to do better than tell them. I had to show them.

I took a deep breath and summoned up all the courage I had. 'I'll answer all of your questions,' I said. My voice came out more steadily this time. 'But first, will you do something for me?'

Saul had a glint of laughter in his eyes. 'You show up out of nowhere, in my land, and demand favours?' he asked.

I nodded. Gulping down my fear, I spoke quickly. 'Take me to the well,' I said.

'The well?' Saul echoed.

'Blue Pool,' Joel said.

'Yes. Blue Pool. Take me there,' I said. 'I need to show you something.'

Saul stared at me. 'Why?' he asked.

'Do what the girl says.' A woman's voice came through the gap in the hut, before I had a chance to answer. She walked inside and came right up to Saul.

'What harm will it do?' the woman asked him.

Her voice was so gentle, I already felt better for her being here. That was when I realised whose voice it was. She was the third voice I'd heard yesterday.

Saul and the woman held each other's eyes for a moment. Their gaze was like a high wire, stretching across the space in a dangerous game of truth or dare, and it locked everyone else out.

Eventually, Saul shrugged. 'Very well,' he said. 'We will do as Ella says.' Waving a hand towards the doorway, he indicated for me to leave. 'To Blue Pool,' he instructed. 'You too, Joel. Let's see what this is all about.'

Joel and I retraced our steps through the forest. Saul followed behind with Ella.

'Want to explain what's going on?' Joel asked as we walked.

'You'll see when we get there.'

'Fair enough,' Joel said.

'Tell me about Ella,' I said.

'She's a good influence on Saul. Helps him make the right decisions.'

'Is she his wife?'

'Ex-wife. They're still good friends. She's kind

of his second-in-command. She helps keep his head straight.'

'She's in his faction?'

'Ella doesn't believe in the factions. She floats above all of it. Never takes any sides. Never makes any enemies. Never raises her voice. She's like the thread that holds us all together.'

'Why isn't *she* the leader?' I asked.

Joel shrugged. 'Good question, I suppose. We've never had a woman leader.'

'Well, maybe it's time you did,' I muttered.

We'd come to the hole in the earth that led down to the pool. 'Right, we're here,' Joel said. 'You ready?'

'I guess,' I replied, and the four of us carefully picked our way down the rocks to the pool.

Something twitched inside me as we reached the bottom and I looked at the water. A mixture of excitement and fear, I guessed. Excitement because, no matter what else happened, the thought of diving into that beautiful pool and transforming into a mermaid made me feel calm.

Fear because I had no idea how they were going to respond.

How was *anyone* meant to respond? First a girl turns up out of nowhere in a land that's supposedly impossible to reach, then she dives into water and comes back up with a tail? They might lock me up for witchcraft or something.

I hesitated by the side of the pool.

Then I remembered the words I'd overheard, the story Joel had told me, the picture around Saul's neck.

If there was even the smallest chance that I could help save all of them, all of us, and goodness knew how many thousands more, I had no choice. I *had* to do it.

I turned away from them, looked down at the clear blue water – and dived in.

As I swam, I felt that familiar feeling start to spread through me from my toes to my knees, electricity running all the way up my legs as they fizzed and tingled . . . and finally turned into my tail.

My heart was leaping around in my chest like a fish gasping for survival on a shore. This was it. Make or break time.

I flicked my tail to get some momentum. Then I kicked as hard as I could, propelled myself high above the water and dived back into the pool with a splash. As I dived down, I flipped my tail into the air as high as I could, swishing and twirling it around, to make sure they would see it.

For a minute or two, I let myself luxuriate in the feeling of being in the pool. When I was in water, it felt like I was whole. Like I was home. Being a mermaid was what completed me.

For a split second, it crossed my mind that

perhaps I could just stay down here. Swim about under the water until they gave up on me and went away. Then, somehow, get through the death chute again, and get back to the hotel. Back to the holiday I was meant to be on.

I could do it.

Except that meant I'd have to pretend to myself that I hadn't been told everything I'd been told.

The Prophecy predicted that I would come – and I had. If it also predicted an earthquake that threatened destruction on a scale like Joel had told me – then I had no choice. People's lives were depending on me.

Not just all the people here on Forgotten Island, but on Majesty Island too. My family, my best friends – and then the thousands more on the other side of the ocean.

I couldn't leave all those people to die.

So I swam upwards, towards the light.

As I broke through the surface of the lake, I wiped my hair off my face and spun round to face the others.

This was it. The moment of truth.

CHAPTER 12

Saul and Joel had identical looks on their faces.

They looked like they were competing to win gold in a who-can-stand-still-with-their-mouth-open-wide-enough-to-catch-the-most-flies-in-it competition.

Ella was the only one who didn't look completely shocked. While the others stood there, staring, sputtering and saying things like 'How?' and 'B-but that's imposs . . .' she walked down to the edge of the pool and sat next to me.

My tail flipped and flickered as I pulled myself

out and sat on the rocks. Bit by bit, the flickering lessened, the scales melted away and my legs returned.

'I had a feeling it was you,' she said.

'What was me?'

'That you were the one,' she said.

I looked at her. 'Really? Why?' I asked.

She smiled as she replied, 'I gave him that necklace.'

I swallowed. 'I just hope I will be able to help,' I mumbled.

'You will, little one, I'm sure. But things aren't as simple as they might seem.'

I wanted to point out that, frankly, things didn't actually seem simple at all. She went on before I had the chance.

'There are other things to account for,' she said. 'And other people. We have a long way to go. A lot of people to convince, and others to find. Do you understand?'

'Um. Not really.'

Ella smiled. 'I'll explain on the way back. Come on.' She reached down to help me up.

I brushed down my legs. As I stood up, Saul indicated for me to approach him.

I stood in front of him and looked up into his dark eyes.

He stared at me for a long time. Eventually, he spoke. 'I don't even know your name,' he said.

I cleared my throat. 'It's Emily.'

'Emily. You should have had a better welcome,' he said. 'Will you forgive me?'

I nearly burst out laughing. I'd turned up on this island and thought he wanted to chase me for dinner, lock me away and guard me with weapons – and he was asking if *I* would forgive *him*?

'Of course I will,' I replied. 'Don't worry about it.'

Saul grinned widely and beckoned us all to get moving. 'Come,' he ordered, a strong ruler again. 'We have no time to waste. Gather all the others. The day has come. We have plans to make.'

Joel stopped him. 'Saul,' he said.

Saul turned to him. 'What is it?'

'I . . . I'm sorry,' Joel said. 'I was wrong. We were all wrong. We should have trusted you. We should have supported you, believed in your leadership.'

Saul reached out to pat Joel's arm. 'You do now,' he said softly. 'That's all that matters.'

Then he turned and led the way back to his house.

Saul and Ella walked on either side of me.

'I should have known – I should have thought. I can't believe I didn't even stop to think,' Saul muttered as we walked.

'It's not your fault,' Ella replied. 'You have many things to think about. You cannot always be expected to see everything.' She looked across me to smile at him. 'That's why you have me,' she said.

Saul smiled back at her. 'Do I?' he asked.

'Always.'

Saul went quiet as we continued to walk. Then, a little way further down the path, he stopped. Turning to me, he held out his necklace. 'I have carried this carving around my neck for five years,' he said. 'The Prophecy brought you here. You have proven me right. The Prophecy *will* save us all.'

Ella touched Saul's arm. 'It didn't bring her here,' she argued. 'Perhaps it *foretold* of her arrival. Perhaps, still, it may be coincidence.'

'Coincidence?' Saul burst out. 'You can't seriously be—'

'I'm just saying, let's take it a step at a time,' Ella urged. 'Maybe Emily *is* the one to help us. But even if she is, you know as well as I do that we still have a huge task ahead of us.'

We'd reached a large clearing with a round hut in the middle of it. 'Come,' Saul said. 'We are here now. Let's go inside. We will tell you more of our story, and show you the rest of the Prophecy's drawings.'

He led the way into the hut. 'And then,' he added as he waved me inside, 'between us, we will work out how you are going to help us.'

I followed Saul and Ella inside. Joel was sent to

gather the rest of the community.

As we took our seats and Saul disappeared to fetch the things he wanted to show me, I tried to slow the thumping in my chest. I wasn't sure if it was fear or excitement. Maybe a bit of both.

Either way, when Ella handed me a drink and said, 'Root of camomile. It helps calm nerves,' I gratefully took it from her and gulped it down.

If my shaking knees were anything to go by, it was exactly what I needed.

One by one, people entered the hut. One by one, they turned to look at me, did a double take, then either scowled or smiled in my direction. I tried to smile back at them all, regardless.

I kept reminding myself that I wasn't being held prisoner. I wasn't here against my will. I was here as Saul's guest.

And every time I felt like running away, I reminded myself of what I knew: that there was an earthquake coming and no one outside of this island knew about it.

How many people would be killed if we couldn't stop it?

If I was the only one who could help prevent this

from happening, there was no way I could turn away from that. I just couldn't, and I wouldn't.

Saul was coming back to the group. His arms were full of large, smooth rocks, lengths of bark, smaller stones.

One of the newcomers jumped up to help him. Together, they placed the objects on a plinth in the middle of the hut.

Saul raised a hand and the room hushed. 'Thank you for coming, all of you,' he said as he slowly turned, making eye contact with each and every one of us. 'Today is a special day.' His turning came to a stop as his eyes reached me. 'We have a visitor. A very important visitor.'

I squirmed in my seat and looked down.

'Not all of us have been of the same mind these last months,' Saul went on. 'But that does not matter now. The debating is over. The talking is finished. Now it is time for action.'

He reached round to the back of his neck and undid his necklace. Holding the stone out in front of him so everyone could see the picture on the front, he said, 'The girl in the Prophecy. The one of land and water . . .' Turning back to me, he said in a deep voice, 'She has come.'

Saul paused while some gasped. Others did more scowling. One person spoke up. 'Saul, what do you mean?' he asked, pointing at me. 'The girl of land and water – you're saying this is her?'

Saul nodded. 'I'm not just *saying* it. I have *seen* it.'

The room broke out in grumbling and mumbling, people all talking over each other until Saul held a hand up. 'Ella,' he said. 'Tell them.'

Ella stepped forward into the centre of the hut. She nodded. 'It's true,' she said. 'She's the one.'

Another outbreak of mumbling and talking.

Saul started to raise his hand again, but Ella stopped him. She walked over to the objects on the plinth. Picking up a rock, she held it up and slowly turned so we could all see it. I craned my neck to look.

It was a picture of the island, the waterfall raging down over the cliffs. At the bottom, clearly visible, was a person. Someone coming through the falls.

I swallowed. The room hushed again.

'Emily is a girl of land and water,' Ella said. 'She came to us through the falls, and again through the chute of water in the tunnels. No one has ever achieved this before now.' She held up a hand to quell any more interruptions. 'Saul is right,' she went on. 'He's always been right. We must follow the Prophecy. And we need to move quickly. Every moment we hesitate is a moment lost to nature's unknown plans. You all know it as well as I do. Every pause gives the earth longer to rumble and shake and crack.'

'What are you proposing?' someone called out.

Ella spoke calmly. 'I propose we study the drawings of the Prophecy before deciding, together, what to do next,' she said.

Once again, the hut was ablaze with noise. Arguing and mumbling, questioning, answering.

Ella went on. 'If you are not willing to put your faith in Saul yet, will you put it in me?' she asked. 'Will you at least stay and listen, be *prepared* to change your views when you have heard more?'

The grumbles gradually ebbed away. 'We will keep an open mind for now,' someone called out. 'But it is up to you to convince us.'

Saul took a breath and stepped into the centre again.

'Thank you,' he said. Then, standing next to the row of objects, and pointing at each one in turn, he added, 'The first job is for me to enlighten Emily – and some of the rest of you – as to the significance of these drawings.'

A man came forward to hold the plinth while Saul talked. Joel changed seats with someone else so he could sit next to me.

'You OK?' he asked.

I held my hands out in a questioning shrug. 'I guess,' I said.

And then Saul shushed the room again, and in

a voice that sounded more regal, more confident than it had done before, he told the story of the Prophecy.

CHAPTER 13

'For many, many years, the pictures we found were passed off as idle sketches,' Saul began. 'Pretty drawings that no one questioned or analysed. It was assumed that people had simply drawn what they saw.'

He held up a rock with a picture of a bridge across a swirling river, woven into an arch that seemed to be made of tree roots. Just like the one I'd seen.

'In recent times, however, *some* of us' – he paused and raised his eyebrows to emphasise the 'some' before going on – 'have come to believe that the etchings came from before an event, not after it. This rock was found before the bridges had been built.'

'Wow,' I breathed. 'I mean, surely that's impossible.'

Joel nudged me. 'I know,' he whispered back. 'That's what I've always thought. It's what many of us thought.' He shrugged. 'I guess we were wrong.'

Saul put the rock down as he continued. 'For a long time, I have believed that these pictures in some way foretold events that were to come.' He lowered his head. 'I know that I have not always been patient with those who disagreed.'

The group shuffled and grumbled in reply. Saul tried to quieten the room, but the voices and the grumbles were becoming louder.

'Why should we believe you?' one man called out.

'Why should we follow you?' a woman asked.

Ella was standing near the door, next to a man with his arms folded tightly across his chest. She reached up to whisper something in his ear. He listened, then gave a curt nod. Ella stepped forward and quietly waited in the centre of the hut.

Gradually, the mumbling quietened down and the shuffling ceased.

'This is a time for coming together,' Ella said

softly. 'No more arguing, no more strife. We all know that we are running out of time. We might have weeks. It could be a matter of days. We don't know. But what we do know is that we will not get anywhere unless we agree to work together. We all know one thing: *lives are at stake.*'

She looked around at the room, silently challenging anyone to disagree with her. No one did.

'Good,' she said quietly. 'So let's listen to our leader.'

Saul gave Ella a quick nod of thanks. She stepped back as he continued.

'Those of us who have spent time discussing this have made various observations. One of the most striking things we found was that there was a marked difference in the frequency of certain drawings. Some appear only once. With most of these, we have yet to find an event worthy of note that they relate to. However, the ones we believe foretell events tend to be repeated over and over. And the more repetitions, the more important the event that they depict.'

Saul lifted another rock and held it out. 'This is among the most repeated of them all,' he said solemnly. As he turned to show it to us all, I examined the picture. At first, I couldn't make out what it was, but as I stared, it became more clear. A cliff, broken in half, right down the middle. One half of it falling into seething water below. People running, others falling into the chasm. An ocean erupting.

'We have found this picture eleven times,' Saul said. 'Eleven identical pictures. I assume that I don't need to spell out to any of you what this picture denotes.'

The silence the room gave in reply confirmed that his assumption was correct.

'Occasionally, we have been puzzled by what we have found,' Saul went on. 'We've seen a drawing of a small island beside our own – when we know there is no such island. Another one shows a fan of light at the end of a tunnel, when our tunnels lead only to the clear pool at the heart of our island.'

'How do you explain those, then?' a man called out.

Saul shrugged calmly. 'One or two unexplained pictures are acceptable for me,' he replied. 'I will be honest with you, though. This one puzzles me.' He reached down to pick up a long piece of bark.

'The drawing does not seem to show anything much,' Saul went on.

I studied the piece of bark. Saul was right. I could barely see what it was meant to be denoting. It didn't look much different from the normal swirls found on a tree's trunk.

'But this troubles me more than the others I've

mentioned. If our theory is correct, this one should depict something of great value, as we have found this picture seven times.'

He picked up a dark, jagged rock etched with an engraving. 'Here it is again. The same pattern. We still do not know what it is.'

The picture was clearer on the rock. I leaned forwards to look more closely as Saul held it up.

My eyes followed the patterns round and round – and that was when my stomach started to swirl with them.

I recognised the pattern. I knew what it was.

I nervously raised my hand in the air.

Saul had opened his mouth to carry on, but Ella noticed me. 'Saul,' she said.

'Can it wait?' Saul replied to Ella without looking at me.

Ella nodded in my direction. 'I don't think so,' she said.

Saul turned to me. 'Emily, what is it?' he asked immediately.

'I know what it is,' I said, my voice coming out in a croak.

Saul's eyes widened. 'Are you sure?'

I swallowed. 'Yeah,' I said.

'You've seen it?' Ella asked.

'I've more than seen it,' I replied, putting everything I had into keeping my voice steady. The swirling, the crashing, the mayhem of the underwater death chute; the spinning, spinning, spinning. I knew it.

I met Saul's eyes and held them as firmly as I could. 'I've been inside it,' I said. 'It's what brought me here.'

If there had been any remaining doubts about the Prophecy in that hut, it seemed my admission went quite a way to clearing them up.

Saul had *reason* to want them to believe him. He had staked his leadership on his belief in the Prophecy. Me, I was an outsider who came to them with nothing. No plans, no opinions, no power and no need to try to convince anyone of anything.

And if the shakiness I felt inside was matched by the shakiness of my voice as I told them all what had happened to me, I guessed they would know I wasn't sharing my story lightly.

'I knew it. I *knew* it!' Saul announced when I had finished. 'This was the only significant picture we couldn't identify as more than an abstract pattern. It was the only one that opened a tiny crack in my mind to let the doubt in. Now I am more certain than ever.'

The response was a round of grudging acknowledgement that turned into mumbles and chatter.

Then the man who had been standing silently next to Ella by the door unfolded his arms and stepped forward. The room hushed instantly.

'Dad!' Joel whispered next to me.

'Saul is right,' the man said. His voice was deep, smooth, certain. 'It's time to put our trust in our leader and follow his instructions.' He held out a hand. Saul grasped it and they shook hands almost fiercely. The man – Joel's dad – turned to the group. 'From now on, anyone who disagrees with Saul also disagrees with me. You hear me?'

Silence.

'Marc, thank you,' Saul said warmly. Marc stepped back into the shadows and Saul spoke again, this time more softly.

'Go back to your day. Sharpen your wits, gather all your resources. Prepare for whatever may lie ahead. Leave us to work out our next steps, and be ready to follow us when we take them.'

The audience responded to his words with an awkward round of applause.

Gradually, people left the hut, until the only ones still there were Saul, Ella, Joel, Marc and me.

Saul indicated for us to gather round. 'OK, we have no time to waste,' he said. 'Ella, take Emily on a walk through the forest, show her the drawings on trees.'

'Will do,' Ella replied.

'Joel, get a full inventory of the Prophecy's drawings. We need to study them with Emily, fill her in on our interpretations of them and arm her as fully as possible with knowledge of what will be needed from her.'

Joel did a kind of salute. 'Got it,' he said.

Saul turned to Marc. 'You and I will work together to sort and order the objects we already have.'

Marc nodded sharply.

'Let's all meet back here in an hour,' Saul said. 'And between us, we will form a strategy. Any questions?'

We all shook our heads. 'OK, go! See you in an hour.'

I left with Ella and followed her along the track that led back into the forest. As we walked, she pointed out trees with odd markings, boulders with lines carved into them. Most of them didn't mean much to me – or to her by the look of it, as she usually moved on quite quickly.

Then we came to a clearing with a large oval boulder in the middle of it. 'You need to see this,' she said. 'This picture, or a version of it, is the most common one of all.'

I followed Ella round the clearing to the other

side of the boulder. 'Here,' she said, pointing at it. 'Like the picture around Saul's neck, this one shows how we knew you could help us.'

I stared at the picture. And yes, at first, I agreed with her. The person on the picture, the tail, the water. It was all there, just like on the stone around Saul's neck.

'How many of these are there?' I asked.

'We have found twenty pictures with this person in them,' Ella replied. 'Unlike the other pictures, they are not all absolutely identical. But they are near enough.'

I took another step towards the boulder – and that was when I saw that Ella was right about the person not being identical. The eyes of the person in this picture were etched more heavily so they looked darker than mine. The body shape was different. The hair was shorter. The tail was a different shape.

'Ella,' I whispered, as I realised what I was looking at.

Ella tore her eyes away from the carving to look at me. 'What?'

'It's not me,' I said, my mind racing. The markings on the tail – I knew those markings. I knew exactly who I was looking at.

'What? Of course it is.'

'No. It isn't,' I insisted. 'The reason why there are twice as many of these pictures is because they are pictures of two different people. I'm telling you, this one isn't me.'

'Well if it isn't you, who is it?' Ella asked.

I took a breath before replying.

'It's my boyfriend, Aaron.'

'Emily has something to share with us,' Ella said as soon as we had all gathered back at the hut.

I explained about the picture and Aaron.

Saul took a heavy breath. 'Well then, we have to get him here,' he said, his words tumbling out in a rush. 'If we're going to stand a chance of stopping this disaster, we'll have to find a way. We need him, just as much as we need you.'

I thought of what I'd been through to end up here. It was awful – I thought I wouldn't survive. And yes, Aaron was a semi-mer like me, but he wasn't the same as me. Maybe he wasn't as strong. Look at how he'd got seasick on that boat. I wasn't sure he'd survive coming through the falls.

Plus, there was the small matter of having completely fallen out with him. Why would he do anything for me right now?

Ella answered the question I hadn't even said out loud. She reached over and put a hand on my arm. 'It's not just for us, Emily.' Ella waited for me to look up and meet her eyes before adding, 'It's for your family. They are in danger. Everyone on the other side of this ocean is in danger. We are talking about thousands of people's lives. You know that, don't you?'

I swallowed.

'We understand how these things work,' she went on. 'We haven't only studied pictures; we've studied science, we listen to nature. We have heard the rumbling, and if the cliff separates in the way the Prophecy warns us, the danger will be enormous. It will cause a tsunami that could threaten every coastline this side of the equator.'

'But . . .' I began. My voice sounded like a tiny mouse. I cleared my throat. 'But what am I meant to do? Supposing I get Aaron and I manage to convince him. Say he agrees. Assuming he manages to get through the falls as well . . .' I looked from Ella to Saul. 'Suppose we manage *all* of that,' I asked. 'Then what?'

Ella looked at Saul. 'Emily needs the *full story*,' she said. 'She's ready. We need to tell her.'

Saul nodded at Ella, then indicated for me to follow him as he went over to the objects that he and Marc had organised.

'These are the main points of the Prophecy,' he said. Pointing at a large, round rock, he said, 'We think this is one of the earliest markings.'

I stepped forward to take a closer look. The carving on the rock seemed to depict a storm. Raindrops covering the top half, a swirling sea below. In the distance, a figure loomed halfway into the sky.

'Who's that?' I asked, pointing at the figure.

Saul looked at Ella. She nodded at him. He took a breath, and then he replied.

'That,' he said, 'is the giant.'

I stared from Saul to Ella and back again. 'The *giant*?' I asked. 'What giant?'

'The giant is at the heart of everything,' Saul replied. 'He appears on many of the drawings.' He pointed at the picture in front of us. 'We believe this one depicts the start of our life here as we know it.'

Joel came over to join us, picking up a piece of old tree bark from the floor as he did. 'This is an early one too, isn't it, Saul?' he said.

Saul took the bark from Joel. 'It is indeed. We've found three of these.'

I studied the carving on the bark. The same man again. This time, he was sitting on the edge of a cliff, tears falling from his eyes, growing bigger and bigger as they fell down a steep canyon.

'We all grew up being told stories about the giant,' Saul explained. 'It is a story that each generation has passed on to the next.'

'They terrified me when I was little,' Joel put in.

'Eat your dinner or the giant will eat you! Don't be late home or the giant will catch you. Work harder or the giant—'

'Enough, Joel,' Ella said. 'Let's not frighten Emily.'

'The giant is part of our folklore,' Saul went on. 'Most generations have believed he is a myth.' He pointed at Joel. 'A made-up figure designed to teach children to behave.'

'But you think he's real?' I asked.

'If the Prophecy is to be believed, he is,' Saul replied simply. 'And thanks to you, we now know more firmly than ever before that the Prophecy *is* to be believed.'

Ella picked up the story. 'Our tales of old say that he suffered a great loss, after which he cried for a hundred years.' She took my hand and pulled me round to look at an obelisk-shaped boulder. Again, the large figure loomed – this time over a waterfall. 'The myth says his tears created the falls. The falls created the clouds that hid our island for so long. And the cycle kept going.'

'If that's the case, how come the falls are still going now the clouds have disappeared?' I asked.

'Good question,' Ella replied. 'This has been the topic of many of our conversations in recent times.'

'And?'

'And the truth is, we do not know,' Ella replied. 'We believe there is something beyond our control going on. Beyond our understanding. Perhaps something magical. And perhaps it is the final key that will allow all to become clear.'

'But we do know enough without it. And we know what has to be done,' Saul added.

'And that involves me and Aaron,' I said. 'And a giant.'

'I'm afraid so, yes,' Saul said as he moved on to another picture that showed the giant lying by a lake. The giant looked as big as the lake itself. 'However the falls were created, the giant is part of our life here, as much as the trees and the birds.'

Ella came and looked over my shoulder at the picture. 'He is the part of our folklore that bridges myth and reality. We have never seen him – but most of us have always believed he exists. Somewhere. And as much as we were scared of his wrath, we have always been comforted by his promise.'

'His promise?'

Ella smiled wistfully. 'The promise is so old we hardly know where it began,' she said. 'But it is at the heart of our life here, it fuels our belief in a future.'

'So, what is the promise?' I asked.

Ella met my eyes. 'That he will return. That he will save us.'

I swallowed hard. 'OK,' I said, my throat tight. 'So, what's the next move?'

Saul beckoned me to the other side of the hut. He pointed at a tree stump that I'd previously thought was just a stool for sitting on. I looked more closely and saw there was a carving on it. It was the most intricate picture of them all.

The left side of the drawing showed a tunnel with a tail disappearing inside it. On the right, someone else was coming out from the other side of it. A wide fan of light shone on them as they came out of the tunnel. It wasn't the tunnel that had led me here and brought me to a pool low down in a well. This one led out to a larger lake and an open forest.

'We always thought this was just one person of land and sea,' Saul mused. 'I thought it was showing this person entering and leaving the tunnels. After what you've told us, I believe it is two. They are on the journey together. A journey that can only be taken by those who can live both on land and in water.'

'Wow,' I said, mesmerised by the picture.

'Here's another one,' Ella said, bringing me a stone with a picture on it.

Two figures. One with a tail.

'We thought it was you,' Ella said. 'But you are right – this is the other person of land and water.'

'Yes, it is,' I agreed. This was definitely Aaron. And the other figure, towering over him, was the giant. The two figures were gazing at each other, a lightning bolt crackling through the middle, like electricity zinging between them.

'We don't know what the lightning bolt means,' Saul admitted. 'Perhaps it is connected to a storm. Perhaps it is merely representative of some kind of energy. But look.'

He reached behind the tree stump and brought out a smooth, flat, round stone. 'We believe this is another scene from the story.'

I looked at the carving on the stone. It took my breath away. An island – this island – ripping down the middle. Stones and rubble all around. People fleeing in every direction, running for their lives. Bridging the gap – feet on one side of the island, hands on the other, body stretched between the two and a face tight with effort – was the giant.

'He's the only one who can save us all,' Ella said quietly. 'You know it, don't you?'

I thought about her question. I wasn't one of them. I hadn't been brought up on these tales. I had no reason to have faith in their prophecy.

No reason except that I had seen it for myself. I had lived it. I was part of it. There was no room in my mind for doubt.

I nodded in reply. 'But what . . .' I began. The question hovered behind my lips. I wanted to ask it, and I didn't. I almost knew the answer – but I wasn't sure I was ready to hear it out loud. What was the alternative, though? Hide from the truth and let the earthquake come? I couldn't do that. Ella was right. There were way too many lives at stake.

'What . . . ?' Ella echoed softly.

I cleared my throat and tried again. 'What is my role?' I asked. 'Me and Aaron. If the giant is the one who's going to save us all, what do *we* have to do?'

Saul turned to me, and then, in a quiet, calm voice that left nowhere to hide and nothing to misinterpret, he replied, 'You have to fetch him.'

CHAPTER 14

Ella, Saul, Joel and Marc gave me a stream of instructions as we made our way back to Blue Pool. That was our starting point: from there, a tunnel would lead us out of the pool and hopefully towards the realm where the giant lived.

They tried to be as helpful as possible, but given that most of what we had to do was about interpreting pictures drawn hundreds of years ago, none of us could be completely sure we would succeed.

What we did know was that we had to find the

giant – and once we had found him, we *had* to persuade him to help us.

'Remember how many people are relying on this mission,' Saul said as we approached Blue Pool. 'You are the only ones who can do it – and thousands of lives are at stake.'

In the back of my mind, questions kept tugging at me. I tried to stop them, but they kept coming.

Would I get back to the other side in one piece? And if I did, and we set off on this mission, what if we couldn't find the giant?

What if Saul was wrong after all? What if there was no earthquake coming? What if I was being sent on a dangerous mission for absolutely no logical reason?

As if she had heard my thoughts, Ella came to my side as we reached the pool.

'Let me go down with Emily first,' she said to the others.

'Why?' asked Saul.

'Just give us a moment, Saul. Please.'

Saul shrugged his acceptance and Ella and I made our way down the rocks to the pool.

We stood on the edge, looking down at the water. 'We believe that everything in nature has an opposite force,' Ella said.

I thought back to my science lessons. Weren't we taught that too? Newton's law of something or other?

'The water goes down a long, long way,' she continued. 'We believe it goes as far down as the mountain you'll be climbing to find the giant goes up.'

'OK,' I replied.

'Blue Pool is in some ways the heart of our island,' Ella went on. 'And yet, it is the one place we cannot go. We can swim *into* the pool, but we can't get beyond it. The tunnel you travelled through and the one you will take from here to continue your journey to the giant – we have attempted them many times.'

'But . . . ?'

'We cannot last more than seconds inside them. They are life-threatening to us – to anyone who cannot breathe in water. You are the only person we have ever met who can survive in these tunnels. You understand?'

'I – I think so,' I replied.

'But anyway, that's not why I've brought you here,' Ella went on quickly. She beckoned me a tiny bit closer to the edge. 'Listen,' she said. 'And watch.'

I leaned over the pool and did what she said. I wasn't sure what I was meant to be listening to, or what I was meant to be seeing. Nothing was happening.

'I can't hear anything,' I said after a moment.

Ella put her finger to her lips. 'It will come

soon,' she assured me.

So we stood there in silence and carried on listening.

The minutes stretched on.

And on.

I was starting to feel a bit silly and was about to ask what exactly I was meant to be listening to when I heard it: a low rumble. It was coming from the pool. From deep inside it.

'Look,' Ella said, pointing at the water. The perfectly smooth surface had broken out into ripples.

'Can you feel that?' Ella asked.

I could. The tiniest shake of the ground below my feet.

Seconds later, it was over.

Ella turned to me. 'We believe the earth's unhappiness lies deep below us, deep below the ocean bed,' she said. 'That is why we feel it only when we can access the lowest points of the island.'

'Like here, because Blue Pool goes down so deep,' I said.

'Exactly. There are one or two other places where the seabed has small holes. To a lesser extent, it has been felt in those places. But none as much as here. It's been getting stronger and more frequent each day. We passed it off as nothing at first, when it happened only once every couple of days and was barely noticeable. But now it happens several times a day.'

'Does everyone know about it?'

Ella nodded. 'We have brought every member of the community here in recent weeks. That's why even those who have not believed the Prophecy have known without doubt that a terrible danger is coming.'

'I see,' I said. And I did. Literally. I saw exactly what she was telling me. Saw, heard, felt it. There was no escaping it. An earthquake was coming – right in the middle of this island. And I knew enough from my geography lessons at Shiprock School to know that everything I'd been told here was true. When it happened, it would surely destroy the island – and such destruction would cause an absolutely devastating tsunami. It could change the shape of the world; it would devastate whole countries. It would kill thousands, if not millions, of people.

'You understand what I'm telling you, don't you?' Ella asked.

'I understand,' I said to Ella. 'I know what I have to do – and I'm ready.'

Joel and Saul had joined us at the rocks next to Blue Pool.

'Last chance, Emily. You're sure you are up to this?' Ella asked me. 'It's such a lot to put on to you.'

What was she saying? That I could back out if I wanted to?

'Just because we know how many lives are at stake – no one can force you to do it,' Ella went on. 'It still has to be your choice.'

I met her eyes and nodded slowly. 'I am ready,' I said. 'I know how dangerous it is.' I glanced between the three of them. 'But I know that if I don't do this – and if Aaron doesn't join me – the consequences will be disastrous for the world. I don't want that on my conscience. Let's do it.'

Ella reached out to squeeze my hand. She didn't say anything. She didn't have to. I could see the gratitude in her eyes.

'And you're clear on everything?' Saul asked. 'No last-minute questions?'

I ran through the plans one last time. We'd been over and over them before we left.

I had to get back to the hotel and find Aaron. We'd decided on going through the pool and tunnels, rather than try to get through the falls again. Both were pretty horrendous experiences, but this one was marginally less so.

Before doing anything else, I had to apologise to Aaron for what happened earlier and hope that he was still speaking to me. I hadn't told these guys about falling out with him and Shona. I was pretty sure both arguments were my fault and I didn't quite know how to explain without making myself look awful. I just had to hope Aaron and Shona would accept my apologies and be as keen to make up as I was.

Once we were – hopefully – friends again, Aaron and I had to get Shona to cover for us somehow, so we could disappear for however long the journey was going to take us. We had to do that tomorrow.

Next, I had to bring Aaron back here, and together we had to swim to the bottom of Blue Pool and find the other death chute, which would lead us *out* of the pool and on to another part of the island. From there, we could climb the big mountain only accessible on the other side of that tunnel. Once up there, we had to find the giant and persuade him to come down, so that when the earthquake hit, he could stop the landslide that would set off a deadly tsunami and destroy the island.

I had never felt such pressure in my whole life.

'One of us will stay by Blue Pool at all times,' Ella said. 'We'll wait for you here and see you off on your journey. Don't be afraid, little one.' She smiled gently at me. I couldn't reply. Too many rocks clogging up my throat. So instead, I just gave her a thumbs-up.

'Good luck,' Joel called as I slipped into the pool. 'Thanks!' I called back.

As I dived under the water and waited for my tail to form, I added silently: *I'll need it.*

Going back through the tunnels was even worse than getting here. This time, the pressure of the water was working against me, as though it didn't want to let me through.

I hung on, swimming harder than I'd ever swum, focusing on the task ahead, on how important it was and how many lives depended on me getting through here. I pushed on. And eventually, I made it through.

Bedraggled and exhausted, I swam upwards, looking for the tunnel that led out of the water.

I couldn't find it.

All the tunnels were filled with water. The walkways we'd been led down by Susannah, the ones I'd run down after my argument with Aaron – all of them were now underwater.

Of course! I remembered Susannah's words as we'd sailed into the tunnel on the boat. It was only on a very low tide that the boat could get in the tunnel. The tide had come up in the time I'd been gone. The tunnel was no longer accessible from the outside.

I swam on, past the quay where the boat had moored, and finally out of the tunnel's entrance.

I was back in the open sea.

I swam up to the surface and gasped in the daylight. Blue sea ahead of me. Unbroken blue sky above me. Rushing falls over to my right. Forgotten Island behind me.

I allowed myself a moment – just one moment – to enjoy feeling the sun on my face, to glide in the smoothness of the still water.

And then I dived down and swam back to the hotel as quickly as I could.

I had a job to do, and there was no time to waste.

I felt as though I'd been away for days. In reality, it had been a matter of hours.

Unless Shona and Aaron had covered for me, my parents would be worried sick. And to be honest, after everything that had happened, I didn't see why they *would* cover for me.

As I swam into the bay, the first person I saw was Millie. She was lying on her deck, reading a magazine and drinking from a large glass filled with ice and something sparkly. She giggled a bit as she spoke to me, so I guessed there was something a bit stronger than her usual Earl Grey tea in the glass.

'There you are!' she said, sitting up and pointing at me as I swam over to her, treading water with my tail just below her balcony.

'I – I – I've just been—' I began.

Millie waved a hand. 'Don't worry,' she said. 'Aaron told us you'd made some new friends and you'd be on the next boat.'

'He did?' I asked.

Millie nodded emphatically, and took a sip from her glass.

'So, did you see any?' she asked.

'See any . . . ?' I echoed.

'Bats, of course!'

'Bats . . . ?'

'In the tunnels. Aaron told us that's why you'd gone with your friends. He said you'd joined a group looking for local wildlife in the tunnels. Said you'd seen a bat. Got any pics?'

'Um. No. I didn't manage to get any pics. But yes. Of course. Bats. Looking for bats. Yes, that was what I was doing,' I faltered, thinking that anyone except Millie would have known I was lying through my teeth.

'And did you see any?'

'Err. Yeah, we saw a few. They were . . . flying

around. In the tunnels. They were, um, sweet. I got the next boat back.'

Millie nodded again and took another loud slurp of her drink. 'Lovely. Right, well, your mum and dad went out for a romantic lunch, and now I think your mum's in the spa and your dad's gone off exploring. You'd better go find your pals. See you at dinner,' she said, and with a wave of her hand, went back to her magazine and her drink.

I set off to look for Shona and Aaron.

I started with Shona's room in the cave below mine. Swimming under the decking of my balcony, I called out.

'Shona!'

Nothing.

I swam a little way inside and called again. 'Shona? You in here?'

An empty echo was my only reply.

I did the same at Aaron's. No one there either. As I swam away, I saw Dad swimming towards me.

Act normal, act normal. You've been looking at bats in the caves. Nothing out of the ordinary.

'Hey, Dad,' I said, smiling as naturally as I could but feeling as wooden as a 300-year-old tree.

'Hey, stranger,' Dad said, grinning at me. 'Did you have a good time in those tunnels?'

'Mmmm, yeah,' I muttered.

'See any?' he asked casually.

I was prepared this time. 'Bats?' I asked. 'Yeah. A few. It was great.'

'Excellent. The kids are down at that underwater playground,' Dad said.

Underwater playground?

A stab of — I didn't even know what it was — jealousy? Sadness? Something not particularly nice, anyway — hit me in the chest. *I* should have been the one discovering underwater playgrounds with Shona. Instead, I'd barely seen her since we got here. She was right: I'd been an absolutely terrible friend.

I couldn't wait to put it right.

As for Aaron — I didn't like the idea of him going off finding special places with someone else, but I could hardly blame him. I'd been about as rubbish a girlfriend to him as I'd been a best friend to Shona.

All I wanted right now was to make up with them and work together with them on what we had to do. I *had* to find a way to make us work as a team again.

But first I had to figure out where they were.

'Oh, you mean the one in . . .' I said to Dad, stalling in the hope that he'd fill the gap.

Luckily, he did.

'Yeah, down there behind the rocky outcrop near West Beach,' he said, pointing vaguely towards the edge of the bay.

'Yes, of course, I know the one you mean,' I said. I didn't feel great about lying to Dad, but he seemed so sure I'd know where they were that I would have felt even worse if I had to admit quite how out of step I was with my best friends.

I turned and swam in the direction Dad had indicated, and hoped I'd figure out where this playground was before they'd left and gone somewhere else.

I found the rocky outcrop that Dad had mentioned and started swimming around it.

On the far side of it, a huge fishing net lined the seabed. Beyond that, two tall rocks had ropes wrapped around each of them. In the middle of the rocks, a massive tyre had been tied on to the ropes, joining them together to make an underwater swing.

Sitting on the swing, laughing, smiling, throwing her hair back, was Shona.

Aaron was behind her, grinning and laughing as he swished his tail and pushed the tyre to make her swing higher.

For a moment, all I could do was stare. My stomach felt as if it was swinging and swirling with the tyre. They both looked so . . . happy. When had either of them last smiled like that at *me*?

I didn't have time to answer my own question, thankfully. A moment later, Aaron glanced across and saw me.

'Emily!' he exclaimed, leaving the swing and swimming over to me. I swam towards them both. I only got halfway to the swing when Aaron reached me and pulled me into a massive hug.

'I'm so glad you're safe,' he said, hugging me even harder.

I hugged him back.

'I've been so worried. We both have,' he added.

I pulled away from him a little. I didn't want to ruin everything straight away by pointing out that they hadn't exactly *looked* worried just now. But I couldn't stop my mouth from mumbling, 'You seem kind of OK, if I'm honest.'

Aaron's face reddened a tiny bit. 'We spent ages looking for you,' he said quickly. 'After you'd gone off, I assumed you'd make your own way back to Majesty Island. We've been swimming all around the island trying to find you. Honestly, Em, we've only just taken a break. We ran out of ideas.'

Shona had slipped off the swing and edged a tiny bit towards me. 'You're not exactly in a position to complain,' she said to me coldly.

I guessed she wasn't feeling quite as forgiving as Aaron. And I couldn't blame her.

'You're right. I'm sorry.' I looked from one to the other. 'I'm *really* sorry,' I said. 'I have been a terrible friend and girlfriend. I've treated you both badly. I've been selfish, thoughtless and stupid.'

Aaron reached out for my hand. 'You haven't been that bad,' he said. 'Don't beat yourself—'

'Let her finish,' Shona interrupted him.

I pulled my hand away from Aaron and swam closer to Shona. 'You're the best friend anyone could want,' I said. 'You're the best friend *I* could want. I'm really sorry, Shona. Please give me a chance to be a better best friend again. Please.'

Shona looked at me for what felt like hours. It was probably only half a minute, but it was long enough for me to imagine my future without her, and I didn't like what I saw.

I felt the pinprick of a tear starting to form behind my eye when she suddenly shook her head, smiled at me and held her arms out. 'Come here, you silly saltfish,' she said and I swam over to her, hugging her as tightly as I could.

'I'm sorry, Shona,' I said again. 'I really am.'

'It's all right. And I'm sorry, too,' Shona said. 'I wasn't all that nice myself.'

I turned to Aaron. 'I was horrible to you too. I'm really sorry.'

'It's OK,' Aaron said. 'I wasn't a very good boyfriend either. I should have understood you were upset. But look, it's all done now. Everything's cool.'

I smiled at Aaron. 'Thank you. So, we're all friends again?' I turned to Shona. 'You and me are OK too?'

Shona nodded. 'Yeah. Course we are. On one condition.'

'Anything,' I said.

'You promise that we can have the holiday we were meant to have, now. No more adventures, no more danger.'

'Shona, I . . .' I began. How could I agree to her condition? I couldn't. But if I didn't, she wasn't going to make up with me.

I thought about what we had to do. The thing was, Aaron and I were the only ones who had to throw ourselves into a dangerous situation so we could help save everyone. Shona didn't have to go anywhere. She *could* relax and enjoy the holiday. And I couldn't bear our making up to be over already. So I did something that was probably stupid.

I smiled at her, and then, closing a door on the bit of my mind that objected to every word, I allowed my mouth to say, 'Of course I agree.'

Shona pulled me into another hug, and for those seconds, I knew I'd done the right thing.

'Making up with you is more important than anything,' I said. 'You're my best friend and you always will be.'

At least that bit was true.

CHAPTER 15

Aaron swam over to join us. 'Let's go over to Sunrise Rocks and you can tell us where you've been and what happened to you.'

'Sunrise Rocks?' I asked.

'I noticed them early this morning. The light hits them at sunrise,' he explained. 'They're just at the edge of this beach.'

So we did what Aaron said. We swam over to the rocks, and as we swam I tried to figure out how to even begin to tell them about the last few hours – never mind tell them what lay ahead. And do all that without Shona falling out with me again.

It felt like an impossible task.

We pulled ourselves up on to the wide flat edges of Sunrise Rocks. As we sat together in a huddle, tails loosely swishing in the warm water, Shona grinned at me.

'OK, now we're friends again, I've got something for you,' she said as she reached into her tail pocket. She pulled out a couple of stones and held them out in front of her.

I had the feeling I knew what Shona was holding out. At least, I hoped I knew.

'Are they friendship pebbles?' I asked. Shona and I had swapped friendship pebbles when we first became best friends. It was like our special thing, a mark of our friendship.

Shona nodded.

'They're beautiful,' I said. 'Where did you get them?'

'It was odd, really,' Shona began. 'I found them yesterday, while I was swimming around in the bay behind the falls, waiting for you to come back. I was just floating around to begin with, passing the time while I waited for you.'

'To begin with?' Aaron asked. 'Then what?'

Shona blinked a couple of times and talked quickly. 'I came across a kind of well in the seabed,' she said. 'Really deep. As I swam over it, the sand on the seabed kind of puffed up, like something had disturbed it.'

'Something like what?' Aaron asked.

Shona shrugged. 'I guess a big fish must have swum by.'

I didn't say anything. I knew it wasn't a big fish at all. But Shona wasn't ready to hear the truth yet.

'The water went cloudy for a second,' she went on. 'Then I saw something happening in the rocks ahead of me. A couple of stones were falling down them; they must have come loose from the shaking. There was a shaft of sunlight beaming on them. They looked kind of magical as they floated down in front of me.'

'They're so pretty,' I said.

Shona looked down at her hand. 'I watched them slipping through the water, twirling round and round as if they were riding an underwater helter-skelter towards me.'

I smiled at that. I'd pointed out the helter-skelter at the fairground one day when Shona was visiting me in Brightport. She said it was the one thing she wished they had in the merfolk world. Pretty much the only thing humans have that she'd ever been jealous of!

'The pebbles spun towards me and I reached out for them,' Shona went on. 'It was like they had sought me out, chosen me.' She grimaced. 'Does that sound stupid?'

'It doesn't sound stupid at all,' I told her. 'It sounds swishy!'

'They feel special anyway, and that's why I want them to be friendship pebbles,' Shona said. She held the pebbles out. 'So, which one do you want?'

'I don't mind; you choose,' I said. I was too happy about being friends again to care which pebble I had.

Shona passed me one of them. I held it in my hand. It was cold and smooth, about half the size of my palm. One side was plain grey. The other had scratches all over it, from being jostled about in the falls I guessed. The scratches looked like a square box with feathery marks along one edge. I wondered how many years it had been jostled about by tides and weather to be scratched and marked like this.

'I'll treasure it for ever,' I promised Shona.

'Good!' Shona grinned.

For a brief moment, I told myself that the three of us were just sitting here, swapping special gifts and sharing the sunshine and the beautiful surroundings. But I knew I couldn't kid myself for much longer.

'Right,' Aaron said. 'Now you guys are best buddies again, how about telling us where you've been?'

I took a breath. Tried to calm my heart rate down. Told myself it would be OK.

And then I began.

I didn't pause to ask if they believed me. I didn't hesitate over the details. I told them everything that had happened, everything I knew, and everything that we had to do.

I avoided looking either of them in the eyes – especially Shona. I barely stopped to take a breath until it was all out of me.

Only then did I dare to make eye contact with either of them.

I'd done my part. What happened next was in their hands.

I held my breath while I waited for them to respond.

And then Shona did.

'I can't believe it,' she said. 'I actually can't believe it.' Her voice had changed. This wasn't the friendship-pebble-sharing voice. It wasn't even the cold voice from this morning.

It was a voice that sounded like disappointment and betrayal.

'Shona, I—'

'Save it, Emily,' Shona said sharply. 'I don't want to hear what you have to say. After everything we've been through, the promises we made – the assurance you gave me *just now!*'

'Shona—'

She barely acknowledged me. 'After *all* that, here we are again. Emily Windsnap has to save the world! Oh, and let's not forget, she needs to drag her two best friends into the greatest danger in order to do it.'

Aaron broke in. 'Hey, hold on a—'

'No, Aaron,' Shona snapped. 'I will not hold on anything.' She turned to me. 'Look around you, Emily. This place is a *paradise*. There's nothing dangerous, nothing threatening. It is just beautiful. Isn't that good enough for you?'

'Shona, it's not that it isn't good enough. It's that it isn't all it seems. This beautiful island we're on is under threat,' I said. My throat burned with emotion. 'Thousands of people's lives are in danger.'

Shona shook her head. 'I just – I can't believe it,' she said. 'I *don't* believe it.'

'I *promise* you it's true,' I insisted.

'Well, you *would* say that, so you've got an excuse to go off on yet another dangerous adventure that you're so desperate to have—'

'I'm not desperate to have a dangerous adventure!' I burst out. 'People are going to *lose their lives* if we don't do something! I'm telling you, it's *true*!'

Shona stared at me. Her eyes were steel. 'And *I'm* telling *you*, I'm done.'

'Done with what?' I asked. I could barely get the words out; my throat felt like it had been squeezed to the width of a thin wire.

Shona held out her arms. 'With all of it. This, you, crazy adventures, danger. Being swept up in your whirlwind. I'm finished. I can't do it any more. She slid down the rock and back into the water. 'I'll cover for you so your parents don't worry, but that's it. From now on, you do your thing and I'll do mine. Let's just get through the rest of the week.'

And with that, she turned away from me. Splishing an arc of glinting droplets with her tail, she dived down and had disappeared before I had a chance to argue.

'Shona, don't go!' I called after her.

A tight circle of ripples was the only reply.

'Hey.' Aaron shuffled up closer to me on the rock and put an arm around me. 'She'll come round.'

I shook my head. 'No, she won't. She hates me.'

'She doesn't hate you,' Aaron argued. 'Just give her time.'

'We haven't *got* time,' I mumbled.

'She said she'll cover for us. That's going to have to

be enough for now.' He shifted so his face was in front of mine. 'Look at me,' he said, tilting my chin up.

I met his eyes.

'I believe you,' he said. 'I believe all of it. We're in this together.'

'Thank you,' I said, my voice cracking slightly with emotion. After the argument with Shona, Aaron's belief in me felt like it put me back together again.

'I will do whatever is needed to help.'

'Thank you,' I said again. We sat there in silence for a few moments, till Aaron cleared his throat. 'OK,' he said. 'Enough of feeling miserable. Are you ready to start talking about what we do next?'

And, much as I would have loved to pretend to myself that we didn't have to think about what lay ahead, and kid myself that this *was* the relaxing holiday it was meant to have been, I knew I couldn't lie to myself.

I couldn't blame Shona for being angry that I'd dragged her into something like this yet again. I didn't blame her for not believing me, for not wanting to be part of it. She didn't *have* to be involved in it.

But I did, and so did Aaron.

'I'm ready,' I agreed. 'Let's make a plan.'

It was the next morning and we were trying to act normal at breakfast.

Considering Shona wasn't speaking to me, and Aaron and I were about to go on a dangerous mission to prevent a world-threatening event from taking place, acting normal was not exactly the easiest thing I'd ever done.

But we got through it, somehow. Shona had at least agreed to go along with the story that we'd been invited to spend the day with some friends that we'd met the day before.

'So who are these friends again?' Mum had asked, frowning as we finished up breakfast.

'Oh, it's Callum and Jennie,' I said, feeling bad about lying to them, but knowing there was no way we could tell them the truth.

'They're great,' Aaron added. 'We were playing with them in the playground yesterday.'

Dad shrugged. 'As long as you're not a burden on them,' he said.

'We won't be a burden on anyone,' I replied. At least *that* much was true.

'And you promise to be careful,' Mum added.

'We promise,' Aaron said, so sombrely it reminded me how important this promise was.

'Why aren't you going, Shona?' Millie asked.

'I just . . . I'm feeling lazy,' Shona said. 'I'd rather stay around here with you. If that's OK?'

'Fine by me,' Millie said.

'Well, I suppose that's all sorted then,' Dad said. 'Have fun!'

'We will,' I replied, even though the words stuck in my throat as I said them. I honestly wasn't sure that 'fun' was the best way to describe the journey that lay ahead.

'And bring us back a memento!' Millie trilled as we got up from the table.

I couldn't help wondering what Millie would make of the memento we were planning to fetch. The only thing we were going to bring back was a giant whose very existence might still turn out to be a myth.

'Will do!' I replied, as Aaron took our plates into the kitchen.

I paused for a moment, as I didn't want to give anything away – but I couldn't stop myself. I went over to Mum and put my arms around her from behind.

'I love you, Mum,' I said, hugging her tightly.

Mum kissed my arm, woven around her shoulders. 'Hey, silly sausage, I love you too.'

Then I went over to the edge of the balcony and knelt down in front of Dad. Wrapping my arms around his neck, I breathed in the familiar scent of him. 'Love you, Dad,' I whispered.

'Love you for always and for ever, little 'un,' Dad replied.

Millie reached for another croissant. 'What's

with all the big goodbyes?' she asked. 'You'd think you were off on a six-month trek round the world, not a day out with friends!'

I kissed her on the top of her head as I passed her. 'Just feeling affectionate,' I said, forcing a lightness I didn't remotely feel into my voice. I didn't want them to get suspicious – or run the risk of them changing their minds.

I looked over to Shona. She turned away.

'Have a good day,' I said.

She nodded. 'Yep, you too,' she replied without looking back at me.

My chest hurt.

But I couldn't dwell on it. We had to get going.

As I went back to my room and gathered my thoughts, I pulled out Shona's friendship pebble. Stroking its smooth surface calmed my nerves. Even if I didn't have her actual friendship, I had this. It would keep me strong, and remind me that when all this was done, our friendship was worth fighting for.

I packed the pebble firmly into my pocket, and then I set off to join Aaron.

Together, we ducked under the water and swam away from the bay, out to the sea and across towards Forgotten Island.

We reached the cave in the island's side, still submerged as the tide hadn't yet revealed it today.

'Ready?' I asked.

'Ready as I'll ever be,' Aaron replied. And so, together, we swam into the darkness of the cave towards the tunnels. As we swam, I hoped and prayed that we were up to the task ahead.

Whether they knew it or not – whether they *believed* it or not – far too many people were depending on us.

Failure was *not* an option.

CHAPTER 16

We swam one by one through the tunnels. Some of it felt familiar, some completely different. I don't know how many wrong turns we took, but I was starting to feel despondent.

I found my way here and back again yesterday; surely I could do it again today?

Aaron had studied his map and guidebook before we came back, and was trying to match up what he'd memorised with what we were swimming through now.

'Em, I think I recognise this tunnel we're in

now from the map,' he said. 'If I understood you correctly yesterday, I reckon it's a bend to the left, a long narrow stretch, a final bend to the right and we'll be there.'

'Sounds good to me,' I said. 'Let's give it a try.'

So we swam on.

'Anything seem familiar to you yet?' Aaron asked.

'Not really,' I replied. 'I wasn't exactly thinking about where I was going last time. I was too busy being stupid and stubborn. Plus, the tunnels weren't underwater then.'

'What about when you came back again?'

'I don't know,' I admitted. 'Everything kind of looked different coming at it from the other side.'

We'd swum into a new tunnel and it was narrowing. 'Wait,' I said.

'What is it?'

'This feels familiar.'

'OK, that's good. Let's keep going.'

So we did. We swam down the tunnel in single file. As the ceiling grew lower and lower, we stretched out our arms ahead of us and streamlined our bodies as much as we could. The ceiling grew so low there was barely room to flick my tail.

'This feel familiar to you?' Aaron called ahead to me as the ceiling dropped down even more.

'I think so,' I replied. 'I remember it got pretty low at one point anyway.'

Had it been quite this low, though?

Just as I was starting to doubt whether we were in the right tunnel, I heard something ahead of us. The sound of rushing water, a channel gushing along like a furious, magical underwater river.

'Aaron! I think we're there!'

We swam on until, finally, we reached the end of the tunnel, and there it was ahead of us. The death chute.

I turned back to Aaron. 'This is it. You ready?'

Aaron nodded. 'Let's go.'

We dived into the tunnel, and within less than a second, it whipped us up in its force, hurling us round and round, closing in on us, thrashing us around. It went on and on and on, until, eventually, just like last time, it spat us out, one after the other, deep into Blue Pool.

I stayed low in the water, looking around for Aaron. I'd come out first. He was behind me, flung tail over head into the pool.

'You OK?' I asked, swimming over to him.

'I – I think so.' He looked a bit green.

I pointed upwards. 'Swim up. Let's get our bearings.'

So we propelled ourselves upwards and broke through the surface of the water together.

'Emily!'

Joel was on the side of the pool, sitting on a rock. He jumped up as soon as he saw us. 'And you must be Aaron.' Joel perched on the edge of the pool and reached out a hand.

'Um. Yeah.' Aaron took his hand and shook it.

'I'm so glad to see you both,' Joel said, smiling broadly. 'Let me tell the others. Ella and Saul are up there.'

While Joel clambered up the rocks to get Ella and Saul, I glanced at Aaron. He was turning slowly round in the pool. He seemed mesmerised by it.

'It's amazing,' he murmured. 'I've never seen water this colour before. It's so . . . blue.'

I laughed. 'Hence its name, I guess.'

A moment later, the others were climbing down the rocks.

'Emily, you made it back!' Ella called to me as she came to the edge of the pool. 'You must be Aaron,' she said, smiling warmly at him. 'I'm Ella, and this is Saul and Joel.'

Aaron did an awkward wave at them all. 'Hi,' he mumbled.

Saul joined Ella at the side of the pool. 'We cannot tell you how grateful we are for what you are doing,' he said.

Aaron shrugged modestly. 'I can't *not* do it,' he said. 'Emily has explained everything. Too many lives are at stake. It feels like – I dunno – kind of our duty, I guess.'

Ella turned to Saul. 'He speaks like one of us,' she said, laughing.

Aaron's eyes sparkled as much as the surface of the water at Ella's words. 'Well, from what Emily has told me, I'll take that as a compliment,' he said.

'It is,' Ella replied.

Joel came over to the edge of the pool and crouched down. 'You both know what you have to do?'

'I've told Aaron everything,' I assured him.

'And we've been over and over it,' Aaron added. 'I reckon we're clear on it all.'

'Right. Well, good luck, both of you.'

Saul reached out to shake our hands. 'We're all depending on you,' he said.

'We'll be thinking of you the whole time,' Ella added. 'And we believe in you. Carry that belief in your hearts, always.'

'We will,' I said, choked.

'Thanks,' Aaron added.

'You ready?' I asked Aaron.

Aaron nodded. He looked different – I couldn't figure out how. In charge, confident, strong. 'We won't fail,' he said to them, 'I promise you.'

And then, together, we turned away from the others, flipped ourselves into a dive and swam down to the bottom of the pool.

Our mission had truly begun.

We swam lower and lower to the bottom of Blue Pool, looking all the time for an opening in its walls. We were searching for the place where a force as strong as the massive rush of water that brought us in here would take us out in a new direction.

Down here there was barely any light, so we had to feel our way around. We were almost at the seabed when Aaron called to me.

'Emily! I think I've found something!'

I swam over to him, and together we ran our hands over the wall.

My hands hit on something that felt different from the other rocks around it. Sharper, rough, with a crack big enough to slide my arm into.

'Swim lower,' I said.

Aaron followed me down. Running my hand down the crack, I felt it gradually widen into something big enough to swim into.

'This is it!' I exclaimed. 'We've found it!'

Aaron was by my side. 'Come on,' he said. 'Let's go.'

And without either of us saying another word, we kicked our tails, slipped into the hole in the rocks, and swam into the darkness.

We'd only been swimming for a moment or two when I heard the now familiar sound: rushing water. Ahead of us was the tunnel that would do the same as the one that brought us here – it would spin us round, shake us inside out, hurl us every which way – but with one difference. This one would lead us to the giant's lair.

Two more strokes and we were there.

I turned back. 'Ready?'

Aaron gave me a thumbs-up. 'See you on the other side.'

And with that, I swam into the mayhem, gave myself up to it and prayed that we would survive.

By now I knew what to expect, so I didn't try to fight it. I shut my eyes and let the torrent's rushing force carry me.

Eventually, the current began to slow. As it did, I opened my eyes.

We were coming to the end of the tunnel. Ahead, I could see an opening.

Beyond it, a shaft of light beamed down like a dusty fan, sprinkling faintly across the opening and lighting up a line of rock on the other side.

A fan of light. That had been in the Prophecy's picture! We were in the right place!

'We've made it!' I called to Aaron.

The closer we got, the brighter the light

became. An intense spot of daylight shining into the blackness that had been surrounding us since we'd swum into the tunnel.

And then, before I could even think another thought—

WHOOSH!

We were spat out of the end of the tunnel into a still, clear, wide stretch of water.

I floundered about finding my fins for a minute.

'Swim up!' Aaron was beside me, jabbing upwards with his hand.

I did what he said and we propelled ourselves upwards. Soon, we reached the surface. I wiped wet hair out of my eyes and looked round, blinking in the daylight.

We were in a lake. A still, peaceful, glimmering lake, surrounded on every side by plants, trees, animal sounds and bird calls. Above us I could see blue sky.

'We're on higher ground,' I said. 'No one's ever made it to this part of the island.'

'The tunnel brought us upwards,' Aaron murmured.

We hovered in the centre of the lake, treading water with our tails, taking it all in.

'Wow,' Aaron breathed in a whisper that was half awe, half fear as we looked around at the unexplored mass of lush green forest.

After the darkness and the closed-in space of

the tunnels, the colour and brightness of the forest took some getting used to.

'I could live here,' he added. I knew what he meant. It wasn't just that it was beautiful. It felt peaceful too.

As I continued to look round, I noticed something. 'Aaron, look!'

Aaron looked where I was pointing. Across the other side of the lake, there was a tall, dark cliff. Running down the side of it, almost hidden in the trees, a waterfall flowed into the lake. Not as big as the falls that we already knew of; these were more like a meandering river.

'The mountain,' I said. 'That's where we have to go.'

As we swam across the lake, I let myself believe that we were simply out swimming together in a beautiful secret forest. Just for one moment.

It was easy at first. The water was warm like a bath, and so clear we could see the rocky floor as we swam. Tiny fish darted around below us. Crabs edged out from their rocky houses to observe the strangers swimming across their sky. The water welcomed us as we swam easily through it.

Too soon, we reached the other side and reality crept back in. We couldn't afford to get distracted.

We pulled ourselves out, waiting for our tails to turn back into legs.

'Look.' Aaron pointed to a cliff face to the left–

hand side of the waterfall. 'Is that a path?'

I squinted to see where he was pointing. There was a break in the rocks, maybe a clearing, leading upwards. 'Looks like it,' I agreed. 'Let's go and see.'

Aaron led the way to the waterfall, and he was right. There was a track through the rocks and trees. It didn't look like it had been used much in a long time. Branches and thorns stretched over it, and rubble and rocks were strewn across it. But it was something.

It was the only thing.

Either way, it was definitely our best shot at getting to the top of the mountain. According to the Prophecy, that was where we would find the giant.

So we clambered across the rocks and over to the path. And then we carefully made our way through running water and over brambles, dodging thorns, branches and rubble, bit by bit scaling the mountain we simultaneously hoped and feared would lead us to the giant's lair.

I sat down on a rock and looked around as I got my breath back. We'd reached the top of the mountain. The climb had been hard, and even more so for the fact that the spin wash in the tunnel on the way here had wiped out most of my energy.

Aaron came over and sat down next to me.

'What a view,' he murmured. He was right. From where we were sitting, we could see out over the whole forest below us, as well as all the way across the plateau.

We could see everything. All of it.

And that was the problem.

'There's one thing missing from the view,' I said.

Aaron lowered his head and nodded. 'There's no giant.'

'Could we have missed him?' I asked. 'I mean, we only took the one path. Maybe there was another one.'

Aaron held his arms out. 'Look around you. We can see everything in the forest. There's nothing. No giant. There's barely any sign of *life*.'

'You're right,' I added, trying to stop myself from feeling utterly hopeless. 'The Prophecy pictures showed him at the top of the mountain. And this is definitely the top.'

Aaron got up and held out a hand to pull me up too. 'Come on, let's look around,' he said. 'Maybe you're right and we've missed something. Perhaps he's here somewhere.'

'Aaron, you don't miss a giant. That's the whole *point* of a giant. He should be big enough to see from *anywhere* up here!'

Still, we were here now and we had to be sure. So we walked around the top of the mountain. It wasn't very big. We'd scaled the whole thing in less than ten minutes. There was no giant.

There was nothing.

Except . . .

'Aaron,' I said, pulling on his arm.

'What?' he replied without turning round. He was still looking around, craning his neck in every direction.

'Aaron!' I said again.

He turned round this time. 'What is it? Have you seen something?'

'I – I'm not sure,' I said. I pointed at something in the distance. Right at the opposite end of the plateau from where we stood. It wasn't a giant. It wasn't even very big. But it stood out from everything else.

From where we were standing, it looked like a wall. Not a very sophisticated or high one. No neat lines of bricks. Jagged rocks of all different shapes and sizes slotted together, squeezed up and balanced precariously next to each other, building up and up in higgledy-piggledy rows.

It was the only thing we could see that had to have been built by someone. The only thing around that nature hadn't naturally allowed to fall that way.

'Wow – is it a house?' Aaron breathed. 'It looks

pretty small from here, though. Not exactly a giant's lair, is it?'

Aaron was right. It wasn't a giant's lair at all. It was probably nothing. Maybe it was just a pile of rocks after all.

But as we stared, I noticed something else. 'Aaron, there!' I said. 'Above the top of it.'

A line of smoke was drifting upwards from the wall.

'What is that?' Aaron asked. 'A forest fire? Someone sending smoke signals?'

I didn't know what it was – but I did know one thing. I'd seen it before. I just couldn't think where.

Wait. Yes, I could!

I reached into my jacket pocket and pulled out the friendship pebble Shona had given me.

'Aaron,' I whispered. 'Look.'

I held the pebble out in front of me, and looked between it and the sight in front of us.

'Whoa!' Aaron exclaimed.

'I know!'

The wall, the line of smoke coming up from the other side – it looked exactly like the picture on my friendship pebble.

'It must be part of the Prophecy,' I whispered.

We knew what we had to do. It might not be a giant's lair, but whatever was over there, it alone stood a chance of being the thing we had come up here to find.

We got up, brushed ourselves down and nodded to each other.

And then, hand in hand, we made our way across the top of the mountain, towards the raggedy stone wall and the perfect line of smoke.

As we got closer, we could see that the wall was part of a building. A tiny building. Nowhere near big enough for a giant to live in. A giant would be hard-pressed to put one foot inside of it.

But a building, nevertheless.

We walked around it. It had four ramshackle walls. Three of them had holes for windows. The fourth had a door made from logs tied together with twigs woven around them.

The smoke continued to rise from inside the building.

'What should we do?' Aaron whispered as we stood outside the house.

'I don't know!' I whispered back. 'Knock?'

And yes, part of me knew that this was the obvious answer. In normal circumstances, if you want to find out who lives in a house and you're standing outside it, you knock on the door.

But here – it just felt so incongruous. Here we were in the middle of an expanse of land at the top of a deserted mountain. The only sign of human life was this dilapidated building. Whoever lived inside was clearly not used to visitors. It wasn't as if they'd be expecting a morning paper.

'What if they don't take kindly to strangers turning up at their door?' Aaron asked, apparently thinking along the same lines as me.

I shrugged. 'What choice have we got?'

And with that, I raised my fist, paused for two seconds – and knocked.

Nothing.

I waited a bit then knocked again, harder this time.

'Clear off, scrounging vermin!' The voice was deep, rough, gravelly. And didn't exactly sound welcoming.

I looked at Aaron. 'Now what?'

Aaron grimaced back at me. 'I don't know! Try one more time?'

'Really?' I whispered back at him. 'You heard him, didn't you?'

'Yes, but he thinks we're some kind of wild

animal. He wasn't telling *us* to go away.'

Aaron shuffled forwards. This time, he was the one to knock. Three sharp raps.

'I TOLD you!' the voice inside boomed. He sounded even angrier. 'SCRAM!'

Next thing we heard was a shuffling sound on the other side of the door.

'He's getting up!' Aaron whispered.

Half of me wanted to run away, get as far from this angry recluse as possible before he saw us. Let him think it *was* a wild animal. Go back down, pretend none of this was happening.

The other half was stronger. The half that knew how many people's lives were depending on us. We *couldn't* run away.

Forcing my breath to keep going in and out of my body, and begging my legs to stop wobbling for long enough to keep me upright, I stood side by side with Aaron, waiting as the shuffling came closer and closer.

I gripped Aaron's hand as the shuffling stopped on the other side of the door.

I swallowed hard and willed myself not to faint as, with a creak and a squeak straight out of a horror movie, the door slowly opened and a face appeared behind it.

CHAPTER 17

*E*verything stopped.

I didn't move a muscle, and nor did Aaron. The air froze around us; the trees below us stopped waving; the sea stopped moving. We were caught in a moment, as if time itself had stopped.

And then the man spoke.

'Who. On. Earth. Are. You.' Those were his words. One at a time. Spoken like a statement.

I stared at the man – what I could see of him – as he hovered in his doorway. He was old. *Really* old. He wore ragged clothes that looked as if they hadn't seen a washing machine in, well, ever. He wasn't very tall – or he might have been, but he was bent over so much his face was at the same level as mine.

Stretching from his face down to his chest, he had a long, grey beard that was as straggly as the twigs lying on the ground. His eyes were so dark and set so deep in his face I couldn't even see what colour they were. They looked like black holes – and they were pinned on me.

His thick grey eyebrows almost joined as the man frowned.

Looking between me and Aaron, he spoke again. 'I said. Who are you?'

Aaron was first to recover. I say recover. That might be an overstatement.

'I – I – we . . .' was pretty much as far as he got.

'We've come to find the giant,' I said. I mean, what else could I say? *Oh, hi there. I'm Emily and this is my boyfriend Aaron, and we were just out walking when we saw your sweet little house, and thought we'd pop by and say hello.*

No, the truth was a better idea. At least, I hoped it was.

The old man's eyebrows knitted even further together as he frowned harder. 'The what?' he asked.

'The, um, the giant?' I repeated, less confidently.

'We were told he lives up here, and we need him because the island is in danger of—'

'There is no giant here!' The man cut me off. He waved a spindly arm out through the door to indicate the surroundings. 'I think you can see that quite clearly for yourselves. Now I don't know who you are, or how you got here, but as I'm sure you've realised, I quite like my own company, so if you don't mind . . .'

'No!' I yelled as the man started to close the door in our faces.

He stopped, mid-movement. 'No?' he said, raising one of his huge, grey, bushy eyebrows.

'You *can't* go. Not after we've come all this way.' My words tumbled out of me. 'The island is in trouble, we all are – even *you* are.'

At this, the man burst out laughing. Bending over even further, he leaned on his knee as he guffawed.

'It's not a joke,' Aaron said, in a voice that sounded like a kid trying to convince his dad that he felt braver than he really did.

Still grinning, the man looked up. His mouth was missing about half its teeth. The ones that remained were yellow and crooked.

'Not a joke. Oh, you're funny,' he said, wiping his forehead with the back of his hand. 'As if I care. As if it matters to me.'

'It doesn't matter to you that hundreds of people

on these islands and thousands more across the other side of the ocean are in trouble?' I asked.

The man cocked his head, as if to think about a puzzle that made no sense to him. 'Why would that matter to me?'

'Or that your own life could be in danger?' Aaron added.

The man burst out laughing again, even harder this time. 'That would be the best news of all!' he said.

'How can you be so uncaring?' I asked before I could stop myself.

The man leaned heavily on his door and poked his face so far out his nose was almost touching mine. I forced myself not to jump back. His breath smelt like a rotting carcass.

'What good does it do to care?' he asked. For the first time, I thought I saw something different in his eyes. Instead of the darkness of his irritation, it looked more like sadness and hurt.

Before I had the chance to say anything, he pulled himself up as straight as he could and went on. 'Now, leave me alone. I am an old, useless man. I have no desire to help you and I have no ability to do so, either. So, go about your day. Go find your giant. Or don't. But whatever you do, remember this . . .'

'Remember what?' I asked, hoping that this would be the moment. The nugget that he would give us to take away, maybe a clue so we could find the giant.

Lowering his voice, he replied, 'Remember that I don't care one tiny little bit what you do as long as you *leave me alone!*'

And with that, he withdrew into his house and slammed the door behind him.

Aaron and I stood in silence for a moment. Then he turned to me.

'I'd say that went quite well, wouldn't you?' he said with a grimace.

The joke broke the tension of the moment, and I relaxed as I allowed myself to laugh. I was still smiling as we moved away and sat on a rock just beyond the house, my shoulders shaking with laughter. Except, I soon realised they weren't shaking with laughter any more. They were shaking with sobs.

Aaron sat next to me and put his arm round me. 'Emily, don't cry. Please,' he whispered, wiping my tears away with his sleeve.

'What else can I do?' I asked. 'There's no giant here. He was our only hope – and he doesn't even exist. The Prophecy was wrong. But how could it be? It hasn't got anything else wrong.'

The more I talked, the more helpless I felt. And the more helpless I felt, the stronger the tears flowed. I leaned on my knees and let myself cry loudly.

'All this way, everything we've gone through – it was all for nothing,' I sobbed. 'We're stuck on a mountain ridge with no one but a grumpy old man for company, who refuses to help or listen or *anything*. Aaron, this is serious. I'm scared, really scared. If we don't find the giant, all the people whose lives are in danger – their lives are on *us*.'

Aaron took his arm from around my shoulder and stood up. 'Wait here,' he said firmly.

I dragged my arm across my face, wiping my nose and cheeks. 'Where are you going?'

Aaron puffed his chest out. 'I'm going to fix this,' he said. 'I'm going to talk to the man again. We haven't come all this way to be sent away with nothing.'

He started to walk away.

'Wait.' I got up and followed him. Holding out my hand, I said, 'We're in this together. I'm coming with you.'

'OK,' Aaron said, nodding. Then he took my hand and, together, we walked steadily back to the cottage.

Aaron knocked on the door.

Nothing.

He knocked again. 'We're not going away!' he shouted.

Still no movement inside.

I knocked. Aaron knocked. We carried on banging on the door, over and over, calling to the man inside until, eventually, it opened again.

Looking wilder and angrier and darker than ever, the man stood in the doorway. 'Which part of "LEAVE ME ALONE" do you not understand?' he bellowed.

Aaron cleared his throat. He hadn't said much to the man the first time round. I'd done most of the talking, and the man had replied mostly to me.

This time, Aaron spoke, calmly, clearly, firmly.

'Which part of "NO" do *you* not understand?' he replied.

The man turned his gaze on Aaron.

'We've come a long way,' Aaron went on. 'We've not had an easy journey to get here, and we will not have an easy journey back.'

The man kept his eyes on Aaron. He looked mesmerised by him.

'A lot of people are going to suffer if we can't help them,' Aaron went on. 'This might be fine with you, but it is not OK for us. So, no. We will not leave you alone. We can't.'

As he spoke, he was reminding me why I liked him so much. Why I loved him. This was the

Aaron I'd fallen for. The one who stood up for himself, who was daring and brave and intelligent. I liked him so much more than the one who kept telling me how gorgeous I was.

I silently willed him on. And silently willed the old man to give us the information we needed.

The man stared at Aaron. 'I'm not who you are looking for,' he said weakly. He sounded like the fight had suddenly drained out of him.

'You might not be who we are looking for, but you are who we have found,' Aaron went on. 'Now, you can ignore us and bellow at us as much as you like, but we are *not* going away.'

They were locked in a stand-off. The man, staring at Aaron so hard his eyes had begun to water; Aaron staring back, chest puffed out, hands on his hips, like he was declaring war on the old man.

And then, into the silence, into the stand-off, something happened.

The man held up a spindly arm, reached out with a bony finger to point at Aaron and said in a whisper hoarse with emotion, 'It's you.'

The moment seemed to stretch out for ever. None of us knew what to do with it.

The man and Aaron were locked in a mutual gaze that was as taut as a wire. It felt so tense it was as though a spark of electricity flowed between them.

The idea felt familiar.

Where had I heard that before?

Eventually, the man waved his finger at us both. 'Stay here,' he growled. 'Don't move. You hear me?'

'Um. OK,' Aaron muttered.

'Good. Right,' the man mumbled back at us. And then he turned, withdrew into his house and shut the door in our faces.

Aaron and I stood exactly where we were.

'Now what?' I asked eventually.

Aaron raised a shoulder in a puzzled shrug. 'I don't know. Stay here, I guess,' he said.

'Yeah,' I agreed.

We stood in silence a bit longer. I could hear rummaging sounds coming from inside the house. A moment later, the door creaked open.

The man stood in the doorway. He had something under his arm. It looked like a piece of bark from a tree.

'You had better come inside,' he said, standing to the side and beckoning us in with a bony finger. 'I've got something to show you.'

I glanced at Aaron. He nodded and we went inside the house.

Calling it a house was maybe a bit of an exaggeration. A small square. Four walls. Three windows and a door. Random objects piled up in the corners. A fire at one side.

'Sit,' the man said.

I looked around for something to sit on. He pointed at the boulders in the corner so Aaron and I took a seat on two of them. The man pulled a log in front of us and bent his spindly legs to sit down facing us.

Only then did he pull the piece of bark from under his arm.

'Look,' he said. He held the bark out high in front of him, right in front of our faces. There was a drawing on it! A picture – just like the pictures from the Prophecy.

Except this one was a close-up.

A man. Maybe the man who was sitting in front of us now. He looked younger in the picture so it was hard to tell – but the eyes looked the same. The same thin mouth, the bushy eyebrows. Yes, the longer I looked at it, the more certain I was that it was him.

But that wasn't the thing that took my breath away.

'You see it?' the man asked, leaning over the picture, prodding it and looking back up at us.

Oh, yes. We saw it.

The man was standing with a boy. Dark hair,

dark eyes, pale complexion. The man had an arm slung around his shoulders. Man and boy were smiling at each other. Their smiles were the same. Their eyes were the same. They looked like family.

And the boy looked like Aaron. It *was* Aaron.

For a moment, there was no sound. Nothing except the occasional crack and hiss coming from the fire in the corner.

Finally, Aaron spoke. 'I don't understand,' he said. 'What does this mean?'

The old man let out a long, slow, whistling breath. He shook his head. 'You know how long I have been here?' he asked. 'You know how many of my questions have gone unanswered in that time?' He made a tutting sound. 'No, of course you don't know,' he went on. 'No one knows. No one cares.'

'I'm sure that's not true,' I offered gently. 'I mean, maybe—'

The man cut me off with a sharp wave of his arm. 'I am resigned to it,' he said. 'You do not have to try to comfort me. I am beyond comfort.' He half smiled, one tiny edge of his mouth curling upwards while the rest of it twitched. 'See, it doesn't matter to me if there is anyone to care. *I* don't care.'

Aaron shuffled in his seat. 'You don't care . . . ?'

'About anything!' the man exclaimed. He laughed, a rattling wheeze that burst out of him like a dart. Then just as suddenly, he stopped laughing and turned serious again. Pulling the picture to his chest with one arm, he reached out to Aaron with the other.

The man touched Aaron's chin with the tip of his finger, lifting his face to look more closely, and in a cracked voice, he said, 'Or at least, I *didn't.*'

Aaron sat tall on his boulder, back straight, face set as he met the man's eyes with his own. Their gaze was identical, and yes, there it was again: the spark, the feeling of electricity running between them.

I suddenly realised why it was familiar.

The picture of the giant and the boy. The jagged symbol between them that no one could explain. It was here in this room!

Except that this old man wasn't the giant.

So what did it all mean? Could it possibly mean that he *could* help us, even if he wasn't who we thought he'd be?

The man let go of Aaron's chin and stood up. 'You want a drink?' he asked.

I glanced at the fire, and the crooked pot on top of it with steam coming from it. I took in a couple of hollowed-out stones that I guessed were the cups. Brambles, weeds, and nettles hung from the ceiling. I tried to imagine what he might be offering us to drink – and decided I could manage without it.

'Um. We're OK, thanks,' Aaron replied for both of us after glancing at my expression.

'Suit yourselves.' The man turned his back on us and shuffled over to the fire. He took the bark with him and balanced it on a wooden table, the picture facing us.

I reached over to take Aaron's hand while we waited, and we sat in silence as we watched the man stir a clump of herbs into his pot, then pour the mixture into a stone cup.

'Right then,' he said as he brought his drink over and settled himself back on the boulder in front of us. 'I suppose I'd better explain.'

CHAPTER 18

'Long ago, I was quite an important man,' he began. 'Important in *some* circles.'

He paused as if waiting for us to disagree with him. I'll admit, it was hard to see exactly in what context this broken old man could ever have been important – but we didn't interrupt.

'Me and my . . .'

The man stopped. He seemed to choke.

'Are you all right?' I asked.

He ignored me. Instead, he took a sip of his drink and spoke again. 'Me and my wife,' he said in a low, steady voice, looking down at the ground.

He paused again, taking a few more sips of his drink before placing it on the floor beside him and folding his hands in his lap.

'I would say that what I am about to tell you might sound fanciful to you, that you may think I'm making it up. An old man's silly stories.' He wagged a finger at us both. 'But I don't think I need to worry about you two.'

'Why not?' Aaron asked.

The man looked wistfully out through a window. 'Out there,' he said. 'I know this mountain like the back of my bony old hand. I know every piece of ground, every tree, every twig. I know every single animal in the woods. I know the water sources, the food sources – I know it all.'

'OK,' I said carefully. 'And . . .'

'I know the waterfalls, the tunnel that is the *only* way out of here. The gravity-defying, life-threatening torrents inside the tunnel,' he went on. 'And you know what that means, don't you?'

Before we had a chance to reply, he added, 'It means I know it is impossible for anyone to get here,' he replied. '*Impossible*,' he repeated, in case we hadn't heard him the first time.

Then he laughed. 'And yet here you are.'

He narrowed his eyes at us. Was he waiting for a reply? An explanation?

'I . . .' I began, but he waved his hand, as if to swat me away like a fly.

'You do not need to explain,' he said. 'Not yet. The very fact of your presence here is enough to tell me that you are already familiar with magical happenings, and that my story will not shock you.'

Neither of us denied it. He was right. He seemed to know us so well, and yet we still knew nothing about him.

'So,' he said. 'First things first. Let's start with my name. I am Jeras.'

'Jeras,' I repeated. It sounded a bit like Gerry – only more important, somehow.

'I'm Emily,' I said. 'And this is Aaron.'

'OK, Emily and Aaron, here's my story. My wife, Fortuna, and I, we worked for Terra,' the old man began. His eyes flickered briefly between us, to see if we knew what he was talking about.

We didn't.

'What's Terra?' Aaron asked, echoing the question in my head.

'*Who*, not what,' the man corrected him. 'Terra Mater is the queen of the land.'

The queen of the land? I had never heard of a queen of the land before. I knew all about the king of the sea, Neptune. I guessed Terra Mater was some kind of land equivalent.

'We were only minor members of the team,' Jeras went on. 'At least, I was. I never had any particularly exciting duties. Anything small and irritating always seemed to be left for me to do. But I worked hard. We both did.'

He stopped to lift his cup and take a sip of his drink.

'My wife had a skill that hardly anyone knew about.' Placing his cup back down on the floor and wiping his mouth with the back of his hand, he added, 'She could see the future.'

I took in what he was saying. 'Your wife – she's the one who did the picture you showed us?' I asked.

Jeras nodded. 'No one knew about her skill, not back then. She kept it hidden.'

'But you knew?' Aaron asked.

'I knew. Yes. And so did Terra. No one else. So my wife rose through Terra's ranks quite quickly. She became indispensable to her. Any decision that Terra needed to make, she would call for my wife, ask her to draw a picture, show her what was to come.'

'And did she?' I asked.

Jeras shook his head. 'She couldn't make predictions to order. She couldn't see the future at the click of someone else's fingers. Even someone as important as Terra Mater.'

'So what happened?' Aaron asked.

'Terra became more and more impatient with her. Demanded she tell her what was coming. One day, in fear that we were both going to lose our jobs and our livelihoods, Fortuna drew a picture for Terra. Told her it was the future, that it answered whatever question was being asked of her that day – I forget what it was, there were so many. She had to come up with something, so she drew. And she said this was Terra's answer.'

'Had she really seen the future?' I asked.

'No. It was a bluff. A lie. It was a mistake. Next day, Terra made a bad choice based on Fortuna's picture, and that was that. We were out of favour, out of jobs, out on our ears. Our brief time in the light of the land gods was over.'

'What did you do?' I asked.

'We survived. We managed, somehow,' Jeras replied. 'It was around the same time as this that we found Fortuna was pregnant. She gave birth to our beautiful daughter and soon we were so preoccupied with our little family that the world beyond the three of us barely mattered.'

'So it all worked out OK?' Aaron asked.

'For a while, yes. The years went by. We were happy enough. Poor, but content. Some years later, our daughter had grown into a beautiful young woman. One day, I happened to meet an old colleague while I was out with her. He said something that put an idea into my mind.'

Aaron leaned forward in his seat. 'What did he say?'

Jeras smiled to himself as he replied. 'He said my daughter could steal the heart of a king.'

For a moment, he appeared to be lost in the happiness of his memory. I didn't want to disturb him. It was the most peaceful he'd looked since we'd been here.

'I believed the man was right,' he went on after a moment. 'And his words stuck with me. At first, I basked in the warmth of the compliment. But we were nearing the end of our reserves. Our lives had grown tough with our poverty. We were always cold, always hungry. We couldn't carry on like that much longer. And so I had an idea that would transform our lives.'

'What was the idea?' I asked.

'It was perfect,' he said, his eyes glistening now as he spoke. 'The idea would bring us back into the favour of the land gods and enable us to branch out and make new connections, too. Our daughter would live in comfort. We would never go hungry again.'

He paused. Clamped his mouth shut.

'What was the idea?' I asked again. And it was strange, because a part of me suddenly knew what he was going to say. It was as if I felt his answer come to me, whispered on the wind, whistling through the window of his tumbledown house, as it slipped into my mind.

And then he said the words and, even though

they confirmed what I was thinking, I couldn't hide my shock at hearing them.

'I decided she would marry Neptune.'

I watched Aaron's face drain of colour.

'You . . . You . . .' he said.

'Don't judge me,' Jeras went on quickly. 'It wasn't as if we sold her into a terrible situation. We gave her the opportunity of a wonderful life – a much better life than the one she had grown up in.'

'Aurora . . .' Aaron said. 'Your daughter was Aurora?'

The man's head snapped towards him. 'You know her name? You have heard the stories?'

What could we say? We had never heard *these* stories. But we knew all about Aurora. The one true love of Neptune's life. The human who broke his heart when she tried to swim to him on her birthday and drowned.

Aaron's ancestor, Aurora: Jeras was her father.

It was almost too much to take in. Jaw open, Aaron stared silently at Jeras. And then, in a small voice like a young child's, he asked, 'Are you my family?'

Jeras stared back at him for a long time. Eventually, with a slight lowering of his head, he replied, 'I think I am, Aaron, yes.'

'Go on,' I said, reaching across to take Aaron's hand in mine. 'Continue with your story.'

Jeras took another sip of his drink, and a long, wheezing breath, and carried on. 'I planned and planned, and worked so hard over those following months. It was all I thought about, all I cared about. I spoke to Terra's people, and finally she allowed me to visit her.'

'What did she say?' I asked. 'Did she go along with the plan?'

'She *loved* the plan! She saw power for herself. She had long wanted to extend her influence beyond the land. I was the broker to a deal that could potentially give her a chance to share authority with the king of all the seas.'

'And what was in it for you, other than your daughter living in comfort?' I asked.

'I told Terra that I would only arrange it if she would let me back into her circle. She said if I could make the deal happen, she would grant me whatever I wanted.'

'What *did* you want?' I asked.

For the first time since he'd started talking, Jeras looked uncomfortable. His face seemed to darken. His eyes flickered as he looked away. 'I wanted power,' he admitted. 'I said to her, "Make me big. Make me powerful."'

'And what did she say?'

'She told me to go ahead. She told me to make the arrangement with Neptune, and said that once I shook hands with him, she would do exactly what I asked of her.'

'A – a business deal,' Aaron stuttered. It was the first time he'd spoken since realising they were related. 'It was a business deal.'

Jeras wriggled awkwardly on his seat. 'I . . . yes. Yes, it was,' he said quietly. Aaron glared at him, face set and hard.

'How did you make it happen?' I asked. 'Did she know?'

Jeras shook his head. 'Not at first. Terra helped me make contact with a few important people. Finally, the contacts led us to Neptune.'

'You met Neptune?' I asked, amazed.

'I was taken out to him on a boat. We met on a secret island in the middle of the ocean. At first, he laughed in my face, roaring, "Don't you know who I AM?"'

Yup. That sounded like the Neptune I knew.

'So what changed?' I asked.

'I showed him a drawing. It was my wife's. She had drawn a picture of Neptune and Aurora together. On their wedding day.'

'Did *she* know about the plan?' Aaron asked. He spoke through his teeth. His hand clenched harder around mine. He was angry, I could tell. I wasn't surprised. This was his ancestor we were talking about – the love of Neptune's life – and we were discovering the whole thing had been a business arrangement.

'She didn't know either,' Jeras said. 'Look, I know you are probably judging me – and there's nothing you can think about me that I haven't thought about myself. There are no words you can call me that I haven't called myself.' He spoke to the floor. 'And there is no forgiveness anyone could offer that I haven't rejected for myself.'

He looked up and met my eyes. 'I will *never* forgive myself,' he said.

Aaron's fingers loosened round mine a little. 'Go on,' he said stiffly. 'What happened next?'

'Neptune fell in love with her,' Jeras said simply.

I stared at him. 'From the picture?'

'Pretty much. He stared and stared at the picture, then he informed me he was keeping it and he handed it to one of his assistants. He also informed me that I was to arrange for him to meet Aurora – and that I was not to tell her we had already met. I was not to tell *anyone* of the arrangement.'

'So they met through you?'

'I engineered it. They met – and the rest was up to them. They fell in love at first sight, everyone could see that. They were married within weeks. It was a blissful time.'

'And the deal with the land gods?' I prompted him.

Jeras looked wistfully away from us. 'Funny thing,' he said. 'It never happened. After that first meeting, Neptune and I never referred to the business arrangement. We never shook hands. It didn't seem to matter.'

'So you never became big and powerful?' Aaron asked.

Jeras held his arms out to point to his surroundings. 'What do you think?' he asked. Then he shook himself. 'But I didn't care, not then. We were content. Aurora was bursting with joy. She gave us a grandchild. Thanks to Neptune and his generosity, we didn't go hungry again. They were happy, happy times.'

'So what happened?' I asked. 'Why did it change?'

Jeras's face clouded over. 'Despite the good outcome, my actions began to eat away at me. Each time I saw the joy on my daughter's face, I thought about how her happiness had come about. I felt I had deceived her and betrayed my wife. I started to have nightmares. Anxiety ate at me. My secret began to destroy me. Even though Terra had never made me powerful, and although it was true love between Neptune and Aurora, *I* still knew what I had done. I knew I had planned to give my daughter away as part of a business deal. I couldn't forgive myself – not until my wife and daughter knew the truth.'

Jeras paused as he took a few breaths. We waited for him to continue.

'It was Aurora's birthday. She was so happy. She and Neptune had some grand plans to celebrate that evening. I couldn't go on feeling such conflict every time I saw her smile – and so I told her. I told them both. Aurora and Fortuna at the same time.'

Another long pause. Then, in a voice so quiet I had to lean in to hear him, Jeras said, 'Aurora couldn't believe it at first. She made me repeat myself three times. Each time, I watched the happiness drain out of her, until it seemed she was a doll made of cloth with nothing to hold her up.'

'And your wife?' I asked.

'She didn't say a thing. She stared at me, looking at me as if she didn't know me. As if I were a stranger. She wouldn't speak to me.'

Jeras paused to take a few slow breaths before continuing. 'Aurora could not take it in. I tried to tell her that even though it had started as a business arrangement, it had become love almost immediately. I told her that I had never received the favours the land gods had promised. That these were no longer important to me once I saw how happy she and Neptune were together. I tried to convince her that Neptune adored her with all his heart. Anyone could see that was the truth – but she no longer believed it.'

Aaron clapped a hand over his mouth. 'That was why she swam to him,' he whispered.

Jeras nodded, lowering his gaze to the ground as he did.

Aaron had always known the history of Neptune and Aurora. I knew it too. Aurora had swum to Neptune on her birthday and drowned in the process. We always thought she had tried to get to him for love. Now it seemed it was out of desperation.

'She ran out of the house,' Jeras went on. 'Said she had to ask him herself. She needed to hear from his lips that he loved her. She said she would never believe another word I said to her.'

A tear fell from his face to the floor. Jeras swiped a hand across his cheek and then, voice almost breaking, he said, 'They were the last words she spoke to me.'

The fire crackled and hissed in the corner of the room as we sat there. I had no idea what to say.

After a while, Jeras stood up. He went over to the fire and threw a log on it. Then he reached down and picked up a large, round rock. He brought it over to us. It had something carved on to it.

'My wife took to her bed when we heard the news, and never again got up,' Jeras said. 'I spent every day trying to explain why I'd done what I had, trying to get her to understand.'

'And did she?' Aaron asked.

Jeras shook his head. 'She wouldn't listen. She told me I was never again to speak to her, lie beside her or come near her unless I could find a way to make things right.'

'And?' I held my breath while I waited for him to reply.

'I promised I would,' Jeras said. 'Promised over and over that I would somehow find a way, even though I knew in my heart that it was impossible. Our daughter was gone. Nothing would ever be right again.' He paused, before adding in a whisper, 'My wife didn't speak to me again. She died a week later.'

'Oh, Jeras,' I said. 'I'm so sorry.'

He held the rock out so we could see the carving. 'I found this beside her in the bed.' It was a picture of a heart — broken into two pieces. 'I buried her beside her favourite lake.' Jeras's voice was a croak.

I glanced at Aaron. A wet track wriggled down his cheek. 'You lost everything,' he said.

'I deserved to,' Jeras replied. 'Terra came to see me with her team of officials when she heard what had happened. She saw my grief and for a moment I thought she would decide it was punishment enough.'

'But she didn't?' I asked.

'The grief of a mere lifetime was not enough for her,' he replied. 'Or for me. She knew Neptune. Knew that he would find out what I had done. She cursed me to live until he forgave me – which we both knew would never happen. That way, I would suffer for longer than a natural lifetime.'

'Wow,' I breathed. 'And that was it?'

'That was it from her side, but even that was not enough for Neptune. He sent people to see me. We had been living here on this island in the middle of the ocean ever since Aurora and Neptune had married. They lived together in a castle not too far away.'

'Halflight Castle!' Aaron exclaimed.

'You know it?'

'It was my home!'

Jeras allowed himself the tiniest hint of a smile. 'Of course it was,' he said softly.

'Are you telling us we are near Halflight Castle now?' I asked.

Jeras lifted a shoulder in a slow shrug. 'Geographically, we are,' he said. 'But Neptune created such magic around that castle, it's almost impossible to find.'

I knew that. I'd only just managed to swim there myself. It was where I'd first met Aaron!

'Neptune and Aurora were very happy there for their brief marriage,' Jeras went on. 'Neptune had found this island not too far across the ocean and

Fortuna and I lived here. There were other people on the island but we kept to ourselves.'

'So, did Neptune's people find you here?' I prompted him.

'They did. They questioned me for hours and I told them what I'd done.'

'You admitted that you'd told Aurora about the deal?' I asked.

'I *welcomed* the chance to confess. I needed to let it out. And anyway, I was beyond caring about myself. I had nothing to live for or care for – there was no punishment that could give me more pain than I was in.'

'So what happened?' I asked gently.

'A few days after the visit, the skies darkened and the sea around us began to rage, huge swells exploding into enormous waves across the beaches. A terrible storm came. Others thought it was just bad weather.'

'But you knew better,' I said. *I* knew better. I knew all about Neptune's power to create a storm at sea when he was in a bad mood. And I knew enough about his feelings for Aurora to know that this was probably the *worst* mood he had ever been in.

'Neptune blamed me totally. He was right to. I blamed myself in equal measure,' Jeras went on. 'He came after me, and when he found me, he threw everything he had at me. Quite literally.'

'What do you mean?' asked Aaron. 'What did he throw at you?'

'It was like a series of explosions. Like cannonballs being hurled across the ocean – only they were made of water. A tirade of bombs, miles wide and built from deep sea swells, ploughed into the island. The first one exploded on the beach near me. I was thrown across the beach by the force of it.'

'Crikey,' I murmured.

'And that was only the beginning,' he went on. 'One after another, the water bombs came for me. Half of me wanted to give up and let them hit me. The other half – I don't know, maybe it was instinct, maybe cowardice. Whatever it was, I ran from them. They chased me up the hill, each one punching a hole the size of a lake into the cliffs, until finally they stopped. I don't know why. I never found out whether Neptune thought he had finished me off, or if the top of the mountain was out of his reach. Or maybe the fire of his anger had simply run its course.'

I knew full well that Neptune's anger hadn't run its course. It was Aurora's death that made him ban marriage between merpeople and humans for hundreds of years. I decided not to tell Jeras this. I didn't want to make him feel even worse.

'Whichever it was, the water bombing had changed life here for good,' he went on. 'Neptune made the island forever inaccessible. Cut it to shreds so the sides of the island were impossible to climb, shrouded it in a cloud that would keep it hidden from the rest of the world, and left behind him the biggest, angriest waterfall the world had seen.'

'With you stuck at the top of the highest mountain,' Aaron said.

'Yes. Cut off from my wife's grave so that I could never even visit her,' Jeras said. 'The fierce torrents in the tunnels were Neptune's final word. The only way off the top of this mountain was a journey that I could never make. His magic ensured that they would always run too fast for anyone to survive them.'

'Did you ever try?' I asked.

'Oh, yes. A few times. Told myself it didn't matter if it killed me, as I had nothing to live for. But thanks to Terra's curse, it wouldn't even do that. Just left me feeling as close to death as you could get, but without actually dying. Plus, whenever I tried to get through, it spat me back out this side again. I couldn't do it.'

He looked at us both. 'Nobody can do it. It's not possible,' he said. 'Which leads me to you two.' Jeras stared hard from one to the other. 'You are my descendant,' he said to Aaron. 'You are also Neptune's descendant. Does this mean what I think it must mean? Are you one of land and sea?'

Aaron nodded. Jeras turned to me. 'And you too?' he asked.

'Yes. We're both semi-mers,' I replied.

Jeras laughed softly. 'Semi-mers. I like it,' he said. 'Either way, your journey here cannot have been easy. And yet you made it anyway. You must be desperate.'

'We are,' I assured him.

'And it wasn't me you even wanted to find. It was – a giant?'

'He is in your wife's drawings,' Aaron said. 'He's the only one who can save the island.'

'Save the island – from what?'

'From an earthquake that is going to kill us all,' I said.

Jeras stared at me; his dark eyes felt as if they were boring holes straight into my mind. Then he got up. 'OK,' he said. 'I have told you my story.' He went over to his fire, poured water from a carved-out shell into his makeshift pan. 'Now I will make some more tea,' he said.

As the pan began to hiss and bubble, Jeras sat in front of us. He reached out to touch Aaron's arm.

'You have given me a reason to care,' he said. 'I have not had that for hundreds of years. So we will drink tea together, and as we do you will tell me your problem. And after that, I will do everything I can to help you find a way to fix it.'

CHAPTER 19

*J*eras was as good as his word. He sat silently while we told him everything, his dark eyes fixed on us as he listened.

Only when we had finished did he speak.

'I understand what you're telling me,' he said. 'I believe you, as well. I too have felt an occasional rumbling and mistaken it for thunder. I too have drawings of my wife's that point to future events. I'm sure that her forecast is correct. All the others were.'

'But?' Aaron said.

Jeras held his arms out wide, to indicate the extent of his house, of the mountain, of everything. 'But there is no giant,' he said simply.

'There *has* to be,' I insisted. 'You said yourself that your wife was never wrong. We've seen the pictures. We need the giant.'

'Listen to me,' Jeras said firmly. 'There. Is. No. Giant.'

He was right. It was time to face the facts.

'So what now?' Aaron asked, his voice rising with panic as he spoke. 'What are we meant to do? Fortuna got it wrong!'

Jeras was shaking his head. 'I don't understand it,' he muttered, almost to himself. 'Fortuna never got anything wrong. She can't have . . .'

'Look,' I interrupted them both. 'Whether she ever got anything else wrong or not kind of doesn't matter now. However it has come about, she got *this* wrong. So we need to forget about the giant. The giant doesn't exist. We can't sit around here discussing the ins and outs of how and why the drawings are wrong. What matters is that there's an earthquake coming and we need a new solution.'

Jeras and Aaron stared at me, identical looks on their faces. If I hadn't been so filled with panic in that moment, I'd have commented on how similar they looked, how touching it was to see him with a father figure like this – but there was no time to dwell on things like that. So instead, I did what I always do when times get hard and I'm trying to figure out what to do.

I got up and started pacing.

Round and round the room. Pace, pace, think, think.

Come on, there must be a solution. There has to be.

I paused my pacing to sit on the floor and twirl my hair around a finger. The other thing I do when I'm thinking.

And that was when I saw it.

In the centre of the room, a huge tree stump acted as a table. The tree stump had all sorts of things piled on it. But it wasn't the objects on top of the stump that I was concerned with. It was a picture carved into the tree stump itself. Low down, near the ground.

I leaned forward to study it. 'Jeras,' I said. 'What's this?'

Jeras got up, rubbing his legs as he slowly straightened them, and hobbled over. Aaron came with him. 'What's what?' he asked.

I pointed at the picture. 'This,' I said.

Jeras peered down at it. 'I can't even see anything,' he said. 'It's a long time since I've been able to bend down that low to the ground and hope to get back up again. Why don't you describe it to me?'

Aaron had sat down next to me. 'Em, it's . . .' he began.

'I know,' I said.

Looking up at Jeras, I told him what we were looking at. 'It's a mermaid,' I said. 'Swimming in the sea, a dolphin alongside her. And in front of her . . .'

'In front of her, what?' Jeras asked impatiently.

'In front of her is Neptune.'

'Neptune is part of the Prophecy!' Aaron breathed.

As he spoke, something clicked in my mind. The one remaining question that Ella said they had never managed to answer. Why the falls kept going.

It was magic.

It was part of a curse.

It was Neptune. And now the Prophecy showed him with a mermaid.

'You've found the answer!' Aaron went on. 'The Prophecy's answer! Emily – you have to get Neptune!'

Aaron was practically jumping with excitement. It was almost infectious. Apart from one thing.

He was wrong.

'Aaron, look at it again,' I said. 'Look more closely.'

He bent down to squint at the picture. 'What am I looking at?' he asked.

'The mermaid. Look. Her tail is different from mine. Her eyes are bigger. Her hair is longer.' I looked at him. 'You know what this means, don't you?'

'I . . . Yes, I think I do,' he said.

'What?' Jeras asked from above us. 'What does it mean?'

I stood up and met his eyes. 'It means that it isn't me who has to get Neptune,' I told him. 'It's my best friend, Shona. And the problem is, we've fallen out so badly that the *last* thing she's likely to do right now is anything that I ask of her.'

'In other words, we're back to square one,' Aaron said flatly. 'The earthquake is coming and there is nothing we can do about it.'

Jeras instructed us to get up from the floor and go back to our seats. 'Now listen here,' he said in a voice that sounded much more firm and strong than earlier. 'You cannot give up – on your best friend, on your mission, on the thousands of people whose lives depend on you.' He pointed a spindly finger at me. 'Emily, you go back to that friend of yours and you do whatever it takes to mend your friendship. You understand?'

I nodded.

'Why did you fall out?' he asked.

I lifted my shoulders in a sad shrug. 'I let her down,' I said. 'I made promises and I guess I broke them. She can't trust me any more. And how can she be my best friend without that trust?'

Jeras sighed. 'Emily, if anyone knows about this kind of thing, it is me. So listen. I'm going to give you the benefit of my mistakes, and then you can do something about yours before it's too late.'

'OK,' I agreed. 'That sounds good.'

'Don't let your friendship fester and die. Don't let your argument slide into a rift. Do not accept her anger as the final word. If Shona matters to you—'

'She does,' I broke in, tears stinging the edges of my eyes. 'She really does.'

'Well, then, learn from me. Don't waste your time trying to explain why you did what you did.'

That was exactly what I'd done. How did he know?

'I am old, and wise,' Jeras said, replying to my thoughts as though he'd heard them. 'Let your friend be right. Your friendship is more important than your insistence that she understand you. Understand *her*. You hear me?'

'I . . .' I was fairly certain I had the gist of what he was saying. I didn't have to keep on explaining to Shona *why* I'd done what I did. All I had to do was see her side of it. I'd hurt her – and I needed to fix the hurt. That was all that mattered.

I held his eyes. I felt as if I was holding his heart. Protecting it and healing it with my own. 'Yes,' I told him. 'I hear you.'

We worked quickly after that. Jeras scrabbled around in his house, talking to himself, pulling on shoes and a coat.

'I'm ready,' he said. 'Let's go.'

'You're coming with us?' I asked.

'I am.'

'But the tunnel—'

'I'll come as far as I can,' he said. 'I know the quickest way down the mountain.'

So we started out together, Aaron and I following Jeras down tracks we would never have noticed, along winding paths hidden between rocks, alongside rivers trickling down the mountain.

We rounded a clump of trees and I was looking down at the ground, watching my feet to make sure I didn't stumble, when it happened.

Jeras was quite a way ahead of me; Aaron was behind me. Suddenly, without warning, Aaron screamed, 'Emily!' and grabbed me round the middle, pulling me towards him so we fell backwards together and I landed awkwardly on his legs.

'What are you—' I began. I didn't finish my sentence. I didn't need to.

I stared in silence as a massive boulder, probably

half my size, tumbled down the cliff face, smashing into the path — exactly where I would have been if Aaron hadn't grabbed me — and hurtling down into the valley below.

The sound made Jeras spin round. 'Are you OK?' he yelled back to us.

'We're fine,' I called back. I pulled myself up and dusted my legs down. 'Thanks,' I mumbled to Aaron, still in shock at what had happened. 'I think you might have just saved my life.'

He pointed up at the cliff face. 'Look, there are more.'

The rock had started some kind of landslide. A trail of smaller rocks snaked down the cliff in its wake.

'Stay where you are for a moment,' Jeras called.

We pressed ourselves against the mountainside and waited till the landslide was over.

Once it was safe again, I looked at the ground around me. It was covered in rubble. A stone larger than the others had fallen right in front of me. As I lifted my foot to move away, I noticed it had something on it. It looked like a sketch.

I picked up the stone — and clasped my hand over my mouth.

'Aaron — look!'

Aaron joined me and I held the stone out so he could see it.

'Wow, that looks exactly like she told it,' Aaron breathed.

Jeras had come back to see if we were all right. 'What is it?' he asked. 'What have you found?'

'It's a sketch from the Prophecy,' I said. 'It fell at my feet.'

Jeras narrowed his eyes to squint at the picture. 'What is it?'

The picture showed a mermaid, swimming with an arm outstretched. Ahead of her, a fan of light, and two stones falling down into her hand.

'It's Shona,' I told Jeras. 'It's something that's already happened.' I pulled out my friendship pebble and held it out. 'This is one of the pebbles in the picture,' I said. 'And it led us to you.'

Jeras breathed out so hard his breath whistled through his teeth. 'We must be quick now. Landslides like this are extremely rare. This isn't good. Come, follow me – and hurry.'

We did what Jeras said, and followed him along the track, picking our way along it even faster now.

As we rounded the next corner, Jeras stopped and looked up at the sky. 'See that.' He pointed above us. It was the middle of the day, but the sky was darkening.

'What is it?' Aaron asked.

'Something is changing. The sky, the air . . . Listen.'

We listened.

'I can't hear anything,' I said after a while.

'Exactly,' said Jeras. 'Where are the birds? Where are the daytime feeders? The insects, even?'

Why was he asking us where the animals were? He was the one who lived here. Surely he would know better than we did.

'They should be here. Calling to each other in the trees,' he said.

The silence felt eerie. 'Where are they?' I asked

He shook his head.

'It's started, hasn't it?' Aaron asked. 'The landslide, the animals disappearing. That's what they do, don't they?' His words came out fast and high-pitched. 'I've read about it. When some kind of disaster is approaching, the animals always know before the humans.'

'They do,' Jeras agreed. 'And yes, you're right. We are running out of time.'

I stared at them both. I didn't have any words. My stomach felt as if it had fallen down the valley along with the rocks.

Jeras spoke quickly. 'We need to speed up,' he said. 'You have to get back before the landslides get worse. First will be the small foreshocks. Sharp, but brief, and very localised. But they'll get stronger and longer, and they'll spread out more and more. Come, hurry.'

Together, we battled through undergrowth and over rubble, and eventually arrived at the lake we'd come through from the tunnel.

The lake had a tree lying across it. It must have fallen with the shaking from the foreshocks. It was edging towards the far side of the lake, floating through the water like a canoe.

As we watched, the ground began to shake.

'Right, that's it! You have to go – now!' Jeras yelled. 'The tunnel is your only way. If that gets cut off . . .' He didn't finish his sentence. He didn't have to.

'But – but what about you?' I asked. 'What will you do when the earthquake hits?'

'Don't worry about me. I'll be fine. Thanks to Terra, I can't die.' He smiled at Aaron. 'And for the first time in many, many years, I have something to live for. I have family.'

Aaron turned to Jeras. 'I don't want to leave you,' he said.

Jeras reached out and touched Aaron's cheek. 'I know, lad. I don't want you to go, either. But you must. Far too many people are depending on the pair of you, and on your friend Shona. It's up to the three of you to fix things.'

'I want to fix *you*,' Aaron said.

Jeras laughed softly. 'I am beyond repair,' he

said. 'Take that intention and put it into the world out there.'

Aaron threw himself into Jeras's arms. 'We won't forget you,' he croaked.

Jeras wrapped his spindly arms around Aaron. 'I won't forget you either. I will live my days more happily for having met you,' he said. 'Both of you.'

Pressing me into a bony hug, he held me tightly for a moment. As he did, the shaking under my feet seemed to have stopped.

'It's subsided,' he said. 'Just a tremor. Early warning. There'll be more of those before it starts in earnest. But it's coming closer – it could happen any time.'

Jeras moved to the side and waved us ahead of him. 'Now go,' he said. 'And don't look back. You know what you have to do. I'll be willing you on with every nerve in my broken old body.'

'Thank you,' I called to him. 'For everything.' And then we did what he'd told us. We dived into the lake and didn't look back.

As the water folded around me, I kicked my legs until I could no longer feel them. Pausing, mid-lake, I waited for my legs to disappear completely.

Come on, come on.

I was impatient for my tail to form.

Finally, the familiar feeling spread through my body as my tail stretched out and wriggled.

I glanced across at Aaron through the water. It

was murky and bubbling with sediment, no doubt stirred up by the ground's shaking.

His tail had formed too. We flicked our tails and swam to the far side of the lake. Feeling our way along the rocks in the murky, watery darkness, we searched for the tunnel's opening.

'It's here!' I called. Aaron swam over, and together we inched closer to the tunnel's entrance. But there was a problem.

The tree we'd seen floating across the lake had made it all the way to the end. And one of its branches was completely covering the hole.

There was no way out.

CHAPTER 20

We worked and worked at the tunnel's entrance, but it was useless. We couldn't shift the branch away from it.

I tried to squeeze past it but the shaking must have loosened some rocks, because just beyond the entrance the cave itself was blocked up. The tunnel was no longer an option.

We were stuck.

'Aaron.'

He didn't reply. He was too busy scrabbling at the rocks and the tree, trying to get past them.

I swam to his side and touched his arm. 'Aaron, we can't get through,' I said.

'But the Prophecy . . . all the people! Jeras said – we have to get back there,' he cried.

'We can't get through the tunnel,' I repeated.

'We *have* to!' Aaron protested. 'It's the only way out of here.'

'I know,' I agreed. But as I spoke, I realised I was wrong. I grabbed his hand. 'Aaron, it's not the only way,' I said. 'We have another chance. Our only chance.'

'What is it?'

'The falls,' I said. 'We'll have to swim down the falls themselves.'

The current in the lake was so strong, something had to be pulling it down. Surely the only thing strong enough to pull with such force was the falls.

So all we had to do was stop trying to fight it. Stop struggling. Go with the current and let it take us.

We were putting all our bets on one possibility. It *had* to be the right one. Whether we would survive it in one piece, I honestly didn't know for sure. But I knew one thing: we literally had no other option.

So we did it. We let go of the tree, stopped scrabbling against the cave, and let the flow carry us away.

The current grew faster, harder. Soon it was flinging us, tail over head, round and round, lifting us up, hurling us around like a fallen tree being lifted and spun round and round in a typhoon.

Across the lake.

Down the mountain.

Towards the edge where the mighty falls hurled themselves over the jagged cliffs.

And then . . .

It threw us – together with however many hundreds of thousands of cubic metres of water per minute it was – into the falls, and down, down, down into the ocean itself. And all that was left to do was pray that we would still be intact when we reached the bottom.

I landed with an enormous splash and was instantly propelled down almost to the sea floor.

I paddled frantically around, trying to get my bearings.

'Aaron!' I gasped.

'Emily!' I heard him call back to me – but couldn't see him through the mass of bubbles and froth. 'Swim up!' he called.

Once I'd figured out which way was up and which was down, I did what he said. Eventually, both of us made it to the surface.

'You OK?' Aaron asked.

'I – I think so,' I replied, panting. I looked around. The falls were behind us.

We'd done it. We'd really done it!

I didn't get the chance to celebrate for very long.

'Aaron, look.' I waved a hand around us. The sea was starting to bubble. It looked like a pan of water coming to the boil.

Aaron's face had drained of colour. 'The earthquake,' he said. 'It's happening.'

'Maybe it's just another of those foreshocks,' I replied, my voice coming out in a squeak.

'Let's hope so,' Aaron replied. 'Come on, let's get back to Majesty Island and find Shona. Whether it's foreshocks or the real thing, one thing's for sure – we haven't got time to waste. She needs to get Neptune.'

Aaron was right. So we swam as hard as we could, ignoring the bubbling on the surface around us that matched the gurgling tremor in our stomachs.

As we swam away from Forgotten Island, the water gradually started to settle. The frothing and bubbling calmed; the current slowed.

Together, we swam into the bay. It looked just as idyllic as ever. As if nothing had happened. The afternoon sun was beating down on the sea, sprinkling it with glinting lights like little diamonds dancing on the water's surface.

We swam towards the hotel. In the distance,

people were playing on the beach. We could hear the sounds of laughter and conversation.

It seemed so incongruous.

How could they be *laughing*? How could they be playing? Did they have no idea what was going on?

I didn't say my questions out loud, but I guess Aaron heard them anyway.

'It hasn't got this far yet,' he said.

'Which means we might still have time to save everyone,' I said.

'If we hurry,' Aaron agreed.

We swam on, till we arrived at the hotel. As we approached, I could see Mum and Millie on their balcony.

We swam over to them. They were both lying on deckchairs. Millie was reading a magazine; Mum looked like she was asleep, her hat tipped over her eyes, a book lying open on her stomach.

As we approached, Millie glanced up. Seeing us, she put her magazine down and sat up. 'There you are!' she exclaimed. Then she shook Mum.

Immediately Mum was awake and bolt upright. 'What is it, Millie?' she burst out. 'What's happened? What's the matter?'

'Nothing's the matter,' Millie said.

How wrong she was.

Mum spotted us as we reached the decking.

'Oh, there you are!' she said, smiling broadly at us both. 'Did you have fun with your friends?'

How were we meant to answer that? There wasn't time to go into it. We had to find Shona.

'Mum, have you seen Shona?' I asked, trying to keep my voice level.

Mum opened her mouth to reply. She was about to speak when it happened.

A rumble.

'What's that?' Mum asked.

'Thunder?' Millie suggested. We all looked up at the sky. There wasn't a single cloud. But the sky had darkened. It was weird – it was still clear and blue, just a darker, deeper shade.

Then it happened again. This time, it was accompanied by a massive wave that came from behind Aaron and me and nearly swept us on to the balcony. Water spilled over the floor and Mum nearly went flying.

'It's not thunder,' Aaron said darkly.

Grabbing on to the railing at the end of the balcony, Mum froze. 'What's going on?' she asked.

My breathing was ragged. 'Mum, we haven't got time to explain. Where's Shona?'

Just then, the sky darkened another shade and I felt something happening below us. The water was starting to bubble again. The balcony was shaking. Mum's face had turned whiter than the railings.

'If it's not thunder,' she said, her voice coming

out as if it was being squeezed through a tiny pipe, 'then what is it?'

I looked at Aaron. He gave me a quick nod, and I turned back to Mum and Millie. 'It's an earthquake,' I said. 'And it's going to get worse.'

The balcony was shaking so much I wasn't sure it was going to last much longer before it collapsed completely.

'Mum, I need to find Shona. Have you seen her?' I asked desperately.

'She – she was here a while ago,' Mum said. 'She went back to her room. Then she came back and told us she had something to do.'

'Where did she go?'

'I – I don't know,' Mum confessed.

'Look after them,' I urged Aaron. 'I need to find her.' I turned back to Mum and Millie. 'Go inside, both of you,' I urged them. 'Aaron will join you inside.'

'What about you, Emily?' Mum called.

'I'll be fine. I need to find Shona.'

Aaron pulled himself on to the balcony. Before either of us could say or do anything else, Mum spun back round.

'Wait!' she said. 'How could I forget? Shona gave me something for you. She asked for an envelope, and she put something in it. Said to make sure you saw it.'

'What?' I asked.

'I don't know. I put it in your room. She said it was important.'

My tail flapped nervously with indecision. See what Shona had left me in my room or look for her in hers? Either way, we were running out of time. Once we found her, I still had to beg her to forgive me, and still had to send her away to find Neptune. All before the earthquake destroyed everything.

It felt hopeless.

Aaron's tail had melted away and his legs had returned. He reached down to me from the balcony. 'Em, come inside with us. Let's check your room first. See what Shona left for you.'

Aaron was right. I clasped his hand, heaved myself up on to the decking and waited for my tail to transform.

Come on, come on!

It seemed to take for ever.

Eventually, my legs returned and I jumped up and ran inside.

Mum opened her arms and pulled me towards her. 'I'm so glad you're safe,' she mumbled into my hair.

The room was shaking.

'We need to get somewhere safer,' Millie urged. Her face was white and her arms were wrapped tightly around her body as the dressing table began to shake. A hairbrush fell to the floor.

'We took too long,' Aaron muttered. 'We're too late to do anything. It's all our fault.'

'Aaron, it's not our fault,' I began. 'We didn't make the earthquake happen.'

Mum turned to Aaron. 'What are you saying? *What's* your fault?'

'Mum,' I began. 'We have to tell you—'

The rest of my sentence was snatched away by a loud crash as a glass of water fell from Mum's bedside table and smashed on the floor. Chairs were crashing around on the balcony.

I pulled myself out of Mum's arms and spoke quickly.

'We knew this was coming,' I began. 'We heard about it and we were coming back to warn—'

'Heard about it?' Millie interrupted. 'What do you mean you heard about it? Heard from who? From where?'

'From . . .'

'It doesn't matter now,' Aaron jumped in. 'What matters is that it's happening, and it's going to get worse.'

'A lot worse,' I added.

For a second, no one spoke. Mum and Millie

were staring at us, matching looks of shock, disbelief and fear on their faces. The floor shook beneath our feet.

'Maybe it's not going to be as bad as—' Mum began.

And then the wardrobe toppled over and broke into pieces.

'Mum, Millie, you have to get out of here!' I yelled. 'And I need to see what Shona left for me.'

'Emily's right,' Millie yelled as she leapt into action. Stumbling towards the door, she called over her shoulder. 'Main building. Get to the lobby. Run!'

With that, she flung the door open and the four of us ran out into the corridor.

It seemed others must have had the same idea as there were people darting out of their chalets and into the corridor, all heading the same way. Clinging to anything they could, they stumbled and bounced from wall to wall as they picked their way along the corridor.

'You go on ahead,' I instructed the others. 'I'll join you as soon as I've seen what Shona left for me.'

Mum turned round. 'Emily, it's too late for that now. It's not safe in your room.'

'Mum, I haven't got time to explain everything, but if Shona said it was important then I *have* to look.'

264

Mum clung to the wall as the building ⬛

'All right,' she agreed. 'But be quick. We'll ⬛

'Don't wait!'

'I am not leaving you,' Mum said fiercely. 'Now go. And *hurry.*'

'Be careful,' Aaron said, grabbing my arm as I turned. 'If anything happened to you, I don't think I could—'

'I'll be fine,' I said, closing my hand over his.

Aaron pulled me towards him and, for just a moment, I let myself take comfort from his hug. Then he turned back to the others as I turned to run into my room.

I didn't need to worry about a key; the door had been shaken open and was half hanging off its hinges, swinging and flapping as I ran through it.

My room looked as if the messiest burglars in the world had been through it. The mattress was half off the bed. Clothes strewn across the floor. Wardrobe hanging open. Chair upside down. Objects everywhere.

I scanned the room. *Where was it?*

And then my eyes fell on something.

An envelope. With my name on it. It had fallen on the floor.

In two paces, I was across the room and grabbing the envelope. There were two things inside it.

The first thing to fall out was a stone. A pebble –

just any pebble. It was the other friendship that Shona had found.

I turned it over, and clapped a hand over my mouth as I realised what I was looking at.

A drawing was scratched on to its side.

It was a picture of Neptune's trident.

My throat constricted so much I wasn't sure how to keep on breathing through it. I reached back into the envelope and pulled out the other thing that had been in there with the pebble.

A thin, white film of seaweed, on which something had been written in squid ink, in Shona's writing. Three simple words.

I believe you.

CHAPTER 21

I put the stone in my pocket and turned to run out of my bedroom.

I was approaching the door when—

BOOM!

I was hurled backwards. Flung across the room.

I stood up and looked round. My bedroom was collapsing! The wardrobe had fallen across the doorway. I'd never get out.

'Emily!' Mum was screaming from the corridor.

'Mum, go to the hotel lobby. I'm getting in the sea!' I yelled back. 'I'll be safer there!'

'm not leaving—'

'Mum, please! Just go! I'll be safe, I promise!'

Without waiting for her to reply, I picked my way through debris to the other side of my bedroom.

My balcony door was still intact. Fumbling with the lock, I managed to get it open and burst out on to the balcony. Without stopping to think, I jumped off and back into the water. My legs fizzed and tingled before stretching out and melting into my tail.

Even then, even amid everything that was happening, the feeling of my tail forming gave me a split second of happiness. It was as if part of me believed that being a mermaid made everything OK.

Well, this time it didn't. Nothing was going to make this OK.

I dived down and swam away from the huts and the jetties, out into the bay.

Pounding through the water as fast as I could, I tried hard not to think about Mum and Aaron and Millie. I desperately hoped they'd made it to the hotel's main building.

Because as I looked behind me, I saw our line of chalets quiver, shake, and collapse into the sea.

I swam harder. Harder than I'd ever swum in my life. Harder than I would ever have known it was possible to swim.

Yes! The main part of the hotel was still standing. Should I swim there or further out to sea?

There was nothing I could do for them now. My best hope was to get as far as I could from the buildings.

So I swam on. And then—

'Emily!'

Dad! He was in the water beside me. He grabbed me and pulled me into a massive hug. 'Thank goodness you're safe,' he whispered into my hair.

The water was bubbling feverishly around us. Behind us, I could see our hotel. Ahead, in the distance, I could just about see Forgotten Island. Jeras was up there somewhere. And Ella, and Saul, and Joel, and all of them.

Please let them be OK.

'Dad,' I said, as a lull calmed the water for a moment. I needed to tell him.

'What is it, little 'un?' he asked.

I was about to tell him. But two things happened that prevented me.

The first was that the sea suddenly erupted. It was different from the frantic bubbling from moments ago. This was more like a dark, huge swell coming into the bay. It lifted us so high I was airborne for a second, and then it dropped us.

Dad grabbed me. 'It's OK, I've got you,' he said.

And that was when the second thing happened.

I thought I was imagining it at first. I rubbed my

eyes and squinted into the strange, semi-dark sky.
A shape on the horizon.

As it came closer, I knew I wasn't imagining
anything.

I knew this angry swell. I knew the sight on the
horizon.

And I knew my best friend, who I spotted
swimming towards us, ahead of a shoal of dolphins
and a golden chariot.

I knew what it meant.

Neptune was here.

Neptune rode into the bay on his chariot, pulled
by his trusted team of dolphins. As he did, the
water in the bay calmed a little. Enough that the
buildings stopped shaking.

Shona was ahead of them.

I looked at Dad. 'I'm going to go and check
on the others while it's calm,' he said. 'Stay with
Shona, OK?'

'I will,' I said as Shona swam over to me. I swam
to join her. Flinging my arms around her, I nearly
cried.

Before she had the chance to say a word, I
remembered what Jeras had told me.

'Shona, I'm sorry,' I said. 'I'm sorry about everything. It doesn't matter why I did what I did; all that matters is that I hurt you. I let you down. I lost your trust. And I will do anything I can to get it back.'

Shona pulled away to look at me. She was smiling. 'What are you talking about, you silly sand eel? *I'm* the one who should be apologising! I've been a *terrible* friend. Sulking and being moody and stopping you from doing what you want.'

'You haven't stopped me from—' I began.

'I have,' Shona said firmly. 'Look. I should never have made you agree to that silly deal. It was what *I* wanted, not what you wanted. You're who you are. You love adventures and mysteries and—'

'I'm sorry. You're right, I do,' I interrupted.

'And I wouldn't have you any other way,' Shona finished.

'Shona, I feel exactly the same way about you. I drag you into things because *I* want to do them. I won't do it again, I promise.'

Shona shushed me with a finger over her mouth. 'Here's the only deal I'm going to make with you. I promise to accept you for who you are and never again try to make you be someone different.'

I grinned at my best friend – at the bestest best friend in the entire world – and said, 'And I promise exactly the same thing back at you!'

Shona held a palm out in front of her. 'Deal,' she said.

I slapped my palm against hers. 'Deal.'

I looked towards the chariot, coming closer and closer. 'How did you find him?' I asked.

'The weirdest thing happened,' she said. 'I was swimming out to sea, wondering where to go, when this dolphin appeared.'

A dolphin! Just like in the picture!

'It swam right over to me, then started swimming away again. It kept looking back at me, then moving on, as if it wanted me to follow. So I did. It led me right out to sea – and guess where to?'

'Halflight Castle?' I suggested.

'Yes! How did you—? Oh, look, it doesn't matter. But yes, he was out there, near the castle. I found him! Begged him to come. And eventually, he did!'

I smiled at my best friend. 'Shona, you are amazing,' I said.

'YOU HAVE BROUGHT ME HERE FOR NOTHING!'

Neptune's voice boomed across the water to us. Conversation over, for now.

'I see NO emergency!' Neptune bellowed.

Shona and I swam over to Neptune's chariot together.

He looked down at me. 'You!' he said. 'I might have known.'

'There *is* an emergency,' I called up to him. 'There's an earthquake. It keeps starting and stopping. I think the worst of it hasn't even happened yet.'

Neptune glowered at me. 'And this is my problem *how*, exactly?'

Before I could answer him, a sound like a clap of thunder erupted – only it came from below us, not above. The sea began to quiver, white horses breaking out all around us, swell lifting us high before crashing back down again. It felt like being caught in the most enormous sea storm ever.

'You have to help!' I cried as a section of headland started to crack. 'Forgotten Island is going to get torn in half!'

'I can do nothing about it,' Neptune replied. 'I am the king of the *oceans*. I cannot control the land!'

Neptune was right. He had no power over land. But he *had* to be able to do something. Why else did the Prophecy bring him here?

'Please, *please*, Your Majesty,' I begged him. 'Take us to the island. There must be something you can do. There *has* to be.'

'I have told you. There is nothing I can do. And I have no need or desire to discuss it any further. Do you think I have nothing better to do than waste my time on you? Do you not know how *big* I am? How *important* I am?'

Something about Neptune's words were jarring a corner of my mind.

Big.

Important.

What was it about those words? Where had I heard them?

Wait! It was Jeras! He had used them – that's what he'd told the land gods he wanted to be!

An idea was forming in my head.

'Neptune, please, take us to the island. I'm *begging* you. Your Majesty. Stop the water. Please. Just for a moment.'

'I cannot stop it. The sea is boiling and raging like this because of the earthquake, which I have no—'

'Not the sea! The falls. Stop the falls!'

Neptune stared at me as if I'd asked him to fly me to the moon for a cup of tea and a piece of cake.

'Stop the falls?' he asked in a calm, deep voice that made me quake even more than his angry tirades. 'And why would I do that?'

'So . . .' I hesitated. No, this was no time for hesitation. The idea in my mind was getting stronger. I knew I was clutching at straws, but right now it was all I had – and was possibly the only thing that could save thousands of lives. 'So the man can get down,' I finished weakly.

Neptune's face turned even darker than the sky. 'The man?' he growled. '*What* man?'

And then it happened. I saw it dawn on him. He looked around, his eyes taking in the surroundings. Maybe his ears processed my words and the two things met up in a part of his brain that I guessed he didn't visit very often.

'Jeras?' he asked, in a tone that I had never heard from Neptune. Quiet, almost scared, almost reverent. 'Jeras is still up there?'

I nodded, biting my lip so hard I tasted blood.

Neptune leaned down so far he almost fell out of his chariot. 'And why in the name of all the oceans do you think I would let *that* man come down here?' he growled.

I held my nerve.

'B-because we're in great danger – Your Majesty,' I stammered. 'And because I think he might be the only one who can save us.'

Neptune stared at me, holding my eyes with his as though he were pinning me on the end of a spear, ready to throw me to the sharks.

'Well then,' he said, and I didn't like the snarl in his voice. 'It seems I have unfinished business, after all.'

He waved his trident again. 'Jump on board, both of you,' he bellowed to me and Shona. We didn't stop to question him. Together, we scrambled to perch on the back of his chariot.

Neptune called down to the dolphins. 'Take us to the falls of Forgotten Island!'

As we sped off through the bay, Neptune called back to us. 'I'll stop the water flowing for one hour,' he said. 'And let's see what crawls down the mountain.'

Approaching the falls in the middle of an earthquake that was tearing up the land and whipping the sea into a tidal wave should have been one of the scariest things I'd ever done in my life.

And yes, it was definitely up there.

But we weren't approaching the falls in any old boat. We were in Neptune's own chariot. The king of all the oceans.

He would solve this. He had to.

As we approached, he held his trident high in the air and called out into the wind.

'I COMMAND THE FALLS TO CEASE!'

The ground was still shaking. Trees were still creaking and bending while rocks tumbled down the cliff face. I held on to the side of the chariot, flicking my tail in the water, and watched as the falls slowed and slowed, and eventually stopped.

He'd done it. Neptune had stopped the falls!

The cliff side was bare. Great chasms were exposed, rocky formations jutting out – round, gaping holes going all the way up the cliff, each one empty and still.

Neptune turned to us. 'One hour,' he growled.

An hour. Even if Jeras didn't come down, maybe it could still work.

Was an hour long enough for me to swim to the rocky bay that was lying there, calm and exposed now the falls had stopped, run through to the other side and fetch Joel and all the others?

Was it long enough for them all to get out?

It had to be!

The ground was still quivering. It wasn't going to be easy, but they could do it. They could get out. And then, together, we could all get away from here. We could beat it. We could all survive.

But what about the rest of the world? The ones on the other side of the ocean whose lands would be devastated when the tsunami caused by the impending earthquake reached them?

What about them?

It was useless.

And as if to underline how doomed we all were, two seconds later the ground began to shake. The sea boiled around us. The rocks tumbled – and with a creaking, cracking sound so loud it was as if the heavens were being torn apart, the cliff began to split in half.

The foreshocks were over. The earthquake had begun.

It was really happening: the devastating earthquake that Fortuna had predicted was unfolding right in front of our eyes.

I had to cover my ears to block out the screeching, creaking, squeaking sounds coming from the cliff as it started to break. It sounded like an animal in pain. It sounded as if the earth itself was crying out in anguish.

I turned to Neptune. 'Do something!'

In his defence, even he had stopped looking as if he didn't care. 'I cannot do anything!' he called back. 'I am powerless against the land!'

If Neptune was powerless, we all were.

Except maybe one person, if the thought that was still scratching at the back of my mind was right.

I squinted at the cliffs in front of us. Movement. From here, it looked like an ant making its way down the cliff.

Was it him?

I rubbed my eyes. It couldn't be. Surely. Could it?

I stared so hard my eyes were soon streaming with salty water. Bobbing about on the furious sea, I tried to hold still enough that I could be sure.

Yes. *Yes!*

The figure grew bigger as he came closer. It *was*! It was him!

Jeras.

I jabbed a finger at the cliff. 'Neptune – Your Majesty – look!' I cried.

Neptune scowled at the cliff, searching for what I was pointing at. And then he saw it.

'HIM!' He raised his trident in the air. 'Servants, I have changed my mind. I cannot face this man. Take me away!' he called.

'No! No – you have to stay. Please!'

'Is it not sufficient that I have saved the man's life – reunited him with a world that he should never have been allowed to be part of again? That is not enough for you?'

'No!'

The idea that had been forming in my head earlier was now rattling around so hard it hurt. Could it work?

Might Fortuna have been right about the giant, after all?

Jeras was nearly at the bottom of the cliffs. He was approaching this side of the rocky bay. The split in the land was chasing him downwards. The cliff side was separating. He wasn't going to make it!

'Please, Your Majesty, I'm begging you,' I cried. 'It's not for him. It's for all of us. Please, Neptune.'

'Please what?' he snapped. 'What do you even want me to do?'

I took a breath, let it out, took another one. Then I looked Neptune in the eyes and said, 'I want you to shake his hand.'

Neptune burst out laughing – a nasty, hollow, cackling laugh. 'I will *never* shake that man's hand. NEVER!'

I glanced across. Jeras had reached the shore. The cliff face was separating so much a V-shape was starting to form down the middle. Any minute now, half of it would fall into the ocean. When that happened, it would surely be the end of all of us – and the end of goodness knew how many other people on the far side of the ocean. How many thousands would lose their lives from the tidal wave such an explosion would cause?

Once the cliff had split, there would be nothing we could do.

I couldn't let it happen. I *couldn't*.

I reckoned we had a matter of minutes. Maybe not even that.

Jeras had pulled off his shoes and rolled up his trousers. He was getting into the water! Was he thinking the same thing I was thinking?

'Please, Your Majesty. I will never ask anything of you again. Just this. Just this one thing.'

Neptune folded his arms over his chest and didn't reply.

Jeras was coming closer. He was swimming over to us!

'*Please*,' I said again.

Still no reply.

And then . . .

'I am here.' Jeras was beside me in the water. Panting and gasping, he swam over to the chariot and looked up at Neptune.

As he spoke, his dark eyes were streaming – with tears or sea water?

'She loved you with all of her heart,' Jeras said, his words coming out as bursts in between sharp, wheezing breaths.

Neptune folded his arms more tightly across his body, swishing his tail angrily from side to side.

'And with all of *my* heart, I wish I could undo what happened,' Jeras went on. 'There is no one on this earth – no one in these oceans – who feels as much regret as I do. We both lost our loves. Both of us lost a wife. I lost a daughter.'

Neptune's arms had loosened a tiny bit. His tail had stopped flicking from side to side so angrily.

Another creak in the cliffs.

'Please. Neptune. We were once friends. I am

sorry. I am more sorry than anyone has ever been.'
Jeras pulled himself half out of the water. Leaning
on the side of the chariot, he reached an arm
up to Neptune. 'Please, Your Majesty. Forgive
me.'

Neptune looked beaten. His body slackened,
his arms hung limp by his side, trident hanging
down from one hand.

'I . . . I don't know if I can,' he said. 'No. I can't.
I'm sorry, but I can't forgive you.'

Jeras nodded. 'All right,' he said. 'I understand.
I tried.'

He started to move away.

'Wait!' I yelled at him. 'You can't go!'

'I've said my piece. There's nothing more I can
do.'

'*What*? Of *course* there is. You have to shake his
hand!'

Jeras frowned. 'What? Why?'

He *hadn't* got it. He wasn't on the same
wavelength as I was at all. He wanted to apologise
to Neptune, and he'd done that – but that didn't
help the rest of us. It didn't help *anything*!

'The story you told us!' I said. 'About Terra.'

'What about her?' Jeras asked.

'She told you that when you shook hands with
Neptune, you would become big, and powerful.
And you never did.'

'No . . .'

'Jeras. What can you think of that is big? That is powerful?' I asked.

I waited as the cogs in his brain caught on. Finally, they lit his eyes up from inside. 'Oh, my gosh,' he said. 'Oh, my word – oh, my—'

He swam back to the chariot. This time, there was no hesitation. He hauled himself over the side.

'What do you think you're—' Neptune began.

Jeras didn't let him continue. 'Shake my hand. Forgive me! Do it – now!'

Neptune stared at Jeras's hand.

'I have suffered more than most,' Jeras said. 'And I deserved every bit of it. But it is not right to cause suffering to so many others. Please, do it now. Say you forgive me and shake my hand.'

Neptune hesitated for what felt like an hour. Eventually, he sighed mightily and said, 'Oh, well, if it means *that* much to you then good grief, all right, I'll do it!'

He reached out towards Jeras. Jeras clasped Neptune's fingers hard in his, and finally, finally, they shook hands.

CHAPTER 22

I t happened before our eyes. We all saw it. Me,
Shona, Neptune. All the others behind us.

Dad had arrived with Aaron. Mum and Millie
were on a boat that the hotel had organised to get
people to safety. Even from further out at sea, they
saw it too.

The people from behind the falls who had
started to come out from the forest. Clinging to
trees, stumbling along rocky edges, they saw it.

The moment Jeras let go of Neptune's hand, he
started to change.

He started to grow.

His body lengthened and widened. His legs stretched up and up and up. Taller and taller, bigger and bigger, soon he was so large I had to crane my neck to see his face. He grew and grew until he was at least ten times as tall as any of us.

Right there, in front of our eyes, the myth of the giant came to life.

Jeras had wanted to be big. He'd wanted to be powerful. And now, at last, he was both. Fortuna's pictures had got *everything* right.

Without a word, he turned. Walking through water that reached his ankles, like a kid wading through a puddle, he strode back towards the mountain. His legs were like ancient trees, and his head now practically scraped the ring of cloud that still clung to the centre of the island like a lifebelt.

He'd taken two steps and was halfway there when the earth rumbled again. Another split in the cliff.

I could see the people from behind the falls gathering. As the ground gave way below them, they gripped on to trees and clung on to each other for dear life.

He was one step away when—

C-R-R-R-E-E-E-A-A-A-K!

Another section of the cliff ripped away. Surely this was it. Any second now, the cliff would be in pieces. Half of it would be in the sea, taking all those people with it. And surely none of us could survive the fallout once that happened?

I was about to close my eyes and pray – I didn't see the point in doing anything else – when Shona grabbed me and said, 'Look!'

I looked. So did everyone else. I couldn't believe what I was seeing.

With two enormous strides, Jeras the giant had got himself halfway up the cliff face that was still standing. Then he threw himself across the chasm in between the two sides, so his feet were still on one side and his arms on the other. Gripping the piece of cliff that was now almost in the ocean, he stretched out across the gap in between, turning his body into a bridge.

The final picture from the Prophecy.

'Come,' Jeras boomed, his voice like thunder. 'Run. Get across, all of you. Quick, before it's too late.'

We watched as, one by one, the people stepped on to his shoulders, ran down his back and along his legs, to safety on the other side.

They nearly all made it.

There were three people still on the other side when the earth let out one final, terrible roar. The sea exploded, the cliff face ripped away, rocks tumbled down – and the final three slipped and fell.

Gripping the cliff with one hand, Jeras let go

with the other and reached out. They landed in his palm. Still gripping the cliff with his other hand, he carefully placed them on his back and held his position while they ran across to join the others.

Even when they were all across, he stayed where he was.

'Why isn't he moving?' someone called.

'Look!' I called up to them. I pointed at the cliff. The crack had reached all the way down to the bottom. A whole section of cliff had come loose; the giant's grip was the only thing stopping it from falling into the sea.

As we watched, he looked back over his shoulder to check everyone had got across. Then, slowly, gently, he pulled himself back up, and carefully placed the loose section of cliff down in the water, as if planting a small tree.

The giant had made a new island! Right next to Forgotten Island.

The one picture from the Prophecy that had remained a mystery – it was coming to life in front of us!

As people in the boat cheered, and the people on the cliff side waved, I turned to Shona and gave her a massive thumbs-up. I couldn't even speak.

The ground was still shaking, but now it was just an occasional shudder rather than a full-on, earth-splitting quake. Aftershocks.

Shona swam to my side. Aaron joined us a

minute later and the three of us threw ourselves into a group hug, jumping up and down in the water.

'You did it,' Aaron said. 'You convinced him!'

I pulled away. '*We* did it,' I corrected him. 'This is about *us*. All of us. Not about me.'

Aaron grinned at both of us. 'Yeah, you're right,' he said. '*We* did it. We saved the day.'

'We did it together,' Shona added.

I looked round at the people jumping and whooping and celebrating and cheering. 'And we survived,' I said. '*All* of us survived!'

Daylight was fading as the final group of people were picked up by the transport that had come to take us away. They'd been sending boats and helicopters for the last few hours.

Mum and Millie had gone ahead. Dad was helping with the clean-up operation. The Majesty Island hotel staff were gathering blankets and hot drinks for the people from Forgotten Island. They were introducing themselves to each other, helping each other, forming the beginnings of bonds with people they had never known existed.

Ella, Joel and Saul had come to join Shona,

Aaron and me at the water's edge, near the rocks between the piece of cliff the giant had planted and the cliffs behind us.

'We'll call it New Island,' Saul said, pointing at the freshly laid rocks. 'We'll come here to give thanks for all that we have.'

'That sounds good,' Aaron said, smiling at Saul.

'Do you want to plant some stuff on it with me before you go?' Joel asked Aaron.

'Yeah, that would be swishy,' Aaron said.

Joel laughed. 'What's swishy?'

'It means, like, a good thing,' I explained.

'I like it.' Ella laughed.

'We shall all use it from now on,' Saul agreed. 'Especially when we are remembering this day.'

'Look.' Aaron pointed at a rainbow reaching across from the cliff out to sea. It looked like a bridge to a new world.

Maybe it was.

Everything looked new. Even the falls themselves had changed. Neptune had held the water back as long as possible, and once they'd started again, they were completely different.

Instead of the angry, ferocious roar, now the waterfall was a stunningly beautiful stream, meandering and trickling through the fissures and cracks as it found a new path, before dropping down in a thin, delicate line into the ocean.

There was just one thing missing from the picture. One *big* thing.

'What's happened to Jeras?' Shona asked as we all stared at the rainbow, lost in our own thoughts.

It seemed odd to think that a giant could disappear – but he had.

'What *has* happened to him?' Aaron echoed.

'We have to find him,' Ella said.

I glanced at Shona.

She smiled. 'It's fine. Go ahead. I'll stay around in the bay.'

'Joel, go with Aaron and Emily,' Saul instructed. 'Ella and I will stay with Shona. No one is to be left alone today.'

'You sure you don't mind if I go?' I asked Shona.

She gave me a warm smile that showed me she meant it. 'Positive. I hope you find him.'

Aaron, Joel and I clambered up to the top of the rocky bay. 'You OK?' I asked Aaron as we walked.

'I don't want to lose him,' Aaron mumbled. 'He's family.'

'We'll find him, my friend. We'll find him,' Joel said, patting Aaron on the back.

I hung back and let the two of them go ahead of me as we picked our way along a path that had managed to stay intact. We clambered over fallen trees; leapt over chasms that hadn't been there before; hopscotched across rubble.

We came to a lake. 'I know this lake,' Joel said.

'But I don't recognise the hill on the other side.'

'What d'you mean, you don't recognise it?'

He shook his head. 'Exactly what I say. It was never there before.'

'Wait – Joel.' I stopped in my tracks, staring at the hill. 'I've seen it.'

'You can't have done. It has never existed.'

'Not in real life. In a picture.'

The giant lying by the lake. Could it be . . . ?

'Joel, can we go and look at it?' I asked. 'Aaron and I could just swim across the lake.'

'Go,' Joel replied. 'I'll wait here.'

Without another word, Aaron and I picked our way down to the lake, slipped into it and let our tails form. Then we swam across to the other side.

I sat on soft green grass as I waited for my legs to come back. The grass was warm. As if it were breathing.

As if it were alive.

We walked around the edge of the hill. The shape of it – it was like a person. Two long stretches at one end, a ridge on either side, a large hump of a body in the middle.

'It's him,' I whispered. 'It's really him.'

We walked to the far end.

The giant's face turned towards us.

'You found me,' he said, smiling softly. 'This is her lake. Her favourite place. I buried her beside it. And now, finally, I have kept my promise. I have made things right. At last, I can once again lie down beside my wife.'

And then he closed his eyes.

Aaron fell to his knees. 'No!' he cried. 'Please – don't go!'

The giant's smile remained as he half opened an eye. 'It's time,' he said. As he spoke, the ground below us moved. Soft green leaves rustled against my back.

'I am with her again now,' he said. His voice was a hoarse whisper. 'Neptune has forgiven me. The curse is over; I am free to leave. This is the end of my journey.'

'No,' Aaron sobbed.

'Let me go,' Jeras said softly. 'I am ready.' As he spoke, the hillside closed in. He was putting an arm around us both.

'I've only just met you,' Aaron said. A tear streaked down his cheek.

'And you have brought me peace at last,' Jeras replied. 'Thank you. It's down to you now. Both of you. Carry on the work you've started. Keep making things right. Promise me?'

'We promise,' we said together.

The soft grass around us fell slowly back into its place on the ground.

As it did, the movement in the hill in front of us slowed. The eyes closed for good, the smile softened into stillness.

While Aaron stayed there, I stood up to collect armfuls of leaves and twigs.

Together, we laid them gently, carefully, on as much of the giant's body as we could reach.

And then we stayed with him until the moving, the breathing, the life inside him finally stopped.

I stood up and reached for Aaron's hand.

'I'm not going,' he said.

'We need to get back,' I said gently. 'The others are waiting.'

He shook his head. 'I'm not going,' he repeated. 'I'm staying here.'

I knelt down beside him. His cheeks were streaked with tears. 'Aaron, there's nothing here now. He's gone. There might be aftershocks – it's too dangerous to stay.'

'Emily, think about it,' he said. 'It's not far from Halflight Castle, where I grew up. The only place I knew till last year. And since leaving there, if I'm honest, I've never truly felt like I belong.'

I tried to reply, but my throat felt clogged up. 'Aaron, *I* don't belong either. Or, I didn't. You're the only person who makes me feel like I belong anywhere.'

He shook his head. 'No. You have your family; you have Shona.'

'You have your mum,' I said weakly.

'Yes. I've been thinking about that, too,' he said. 'She's coming with me. She belongs here. We both do. Emily, you know it's true. My roots are here, my family.'

'But . . .'

'I can't bear the thought of leaving you – but I have to do it. I have only just met Joel, Ella and Saul, and yet I feel so close to them already. They feel like family. Emily, I want to be part of rebuilding this community.'

As he spoke, I could see it all. Those things he'd said when we had that argument, about it always having to be about me. Well, maybe some things *had* been about me. But this wasn't one of them, and I had to accept what he was telling me.

'You're right,' I said, my voice squeezing through the tears scratching at my throat. 'It's about you this time.'

He pulled me into a hug. 'Thank you,' he whispered.

I held on to him, buried my tears in his shoulder. I had to let him go. He belonged here.

'But come back with us first,' I said, when I could trust myself to speak again. 'We'll get your mum. We'll talk to everyone. We'll help you plan.'

Aaron nodded. 'And you'll visit?'

The rock twisted round in my throat, lodging itself even more firmly. 'Of course I will,' I managed to squeeze out. 'Just try and stop me.'

Eventually, Aaron pulled out of the hug and let go of me. He reached up to kiss the giant's head. 'See you soon,' he whispered.

Then he stood up and took my hand.

We walked back to the lake, swam across it and trekked through the paths. Aaron and Joel talked excitedly all the way. I hung back, smiling as I listened to them and watched them.

'We'll make this hill a special place,' Joel said.

'We could call it Giant's Lair,' Aaron replied.

'We'll rebuild the island,' Joel said.

'We'll work with the people from Majesty Island to make it a place that people will visit from all over the world,' Aaron added.

'But on our terms,' Joel said.

'Absolutely!' Aaron replied.

'And we'll have protected conservation areas and nature trails. We'll rebuild this community.'

Aaron stopped walking and looked Joel in the eyes. 'I will join you,' he said. 'I will help you with it all. I will be part of the community.'

Joel looked back at Aaron and laughed. 'You already are, brother,' he said, slapping him on the back and running off. 'You already are.'

I smiled as I watched them chase each other down the track.

I could see it all. The new world that awaited this island was going to be incredible. It would never be a hidden, forgotten world again.

And so we headed back, and as the daylight faded, Shona, Aaron and I said goodbye to Saul, Ella and Joel, with hugs and thanks and promises of imminent reunions.

And then we joined the others at the boat that would take us away from here. The three of us swam along behind it as we slowly edged out of the bay.

Together, we floated on our backs, watching the island grow smaller and smaller and smaller, until it was just a speck on the horizon.

As we turned away from the island with a broken past and an uncertain future, there was one thing we knew for sure.

That no matter what lay ahead, the bonds of friendship would be as strong as the bonds of the tree-root bridges built generations ago.

They might stretch across chasms. They might even extend over oceans. But they would never, *ever* break.